CELINE

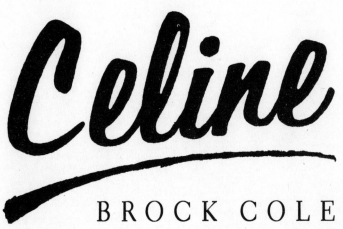

Celine

BROCK COLE

A Sunburst Book

Farrar, Straus and Giroux

For Amy Hosler
1967–1987

CELINE

O N E /

That day I walk home from school carrying *Test Patterns*, the great painting of my junior year, which has hung for a week outside the principal's office and might have stayed there until the end of the term, but someone had written "sucks" after my name in the lower right-hand corner. I'm upset, but I won't paint it out the way Miss Denver wants me to. I don't know why. I have this idea that some restorer in the future might strip away the patch and see it. What difference would that make? I'm not sure. Perhaps I don't want this to be one of my secrets.

I have to walk because the driver won't let me take *Test Patterns* on the bus. There is a strong wind from off the lake, and at every intersection it tries to tear the painting out of my hands. Sometimes it almost lifts me into the air. The stretchers break, first one, and then another, right in the middle. The brown paper wrapping begins to shred into feathery little strips.

(4)

"Hey, white! You trying to fly?" a girl yells at me outside the Projects, and I say, "Yes! Yes, I am," because I see that she is smiling. Maybe I am, at that, because I'm running and flapping the halves of *Test Patterns* like great wings.

It's coming apart, but I don't care. When I reach the building where Catherine and I are living, it is a total mess. Paint cracked, canvas pleated, the stretchers busted and sharp as broken bones. I am happy.

I'm about to fly the painting right into the dumpster in the alley; but no, I think, I must examine it calmly, like a car crash, and so I bundle it into a big wad and carry it up three flights of stairs to the loft that my father has sublet for the year.

There is a little boy sitting on the top step, and he squeezes over to let me and *Test Patterns* by.

"Hi," I say, but he doesn't answer. Not supposed to talk to strangers. He gets up and walks to the door opposite my own to show me that he isn't simply casing the joint, and as I fumble with my keys he keeps his hand on the doorknob as if he's going to open it any second now.

When I pop out again to gather up the pieces of *Test Patterns* which are trying to get away back down the stairs, he's sitting down again, just where I first saw him.

"Caught ya," I say, and he blushes, his big stuck-out

ears most of all. "Are you looking for somebody?" I ask, because he isn't playing. He doesn't look as if he even knows how to play.

"No. I live there." He twists around and points at the (5) big door across the hall. It is gray metal and has four different locks. As I think about it, I realize that I have seen him before—a short person usually standing behind somebody in a skirt.

While I walk around duck-fashion, picking up scraps of brown paper and splinters, he makes himself useful by pointing out all the little bits that I'm missing.

"Thanks. Thanks a lot," I say.

"You're welcome," he says, so seriously that I am sorry all at once that I was being sarcastic. I smile to show him I didn't mean it.

"Can I use your telephone?" he says.

I say of course, and leave the door to the loft open so he can wander in by himself. The phone is on the wall next to the doorway and he can run for it in case I try to grab him while he talks.

I hear him say, "I got locked out," but don't pay much attention after that, because I am busy spreading out *Test Patterns* and thinking about the cracks and holes and wondering if they don't in fact make it better than it was before. I even begin to look kindly on "Celine Morienval sucks," and am about to get out a Magic Marker of my own and add a few more comments about Celine and what she does and doesn't do, when the boy says, "Can my mom talk to you?"

When I take the receiver, I hear a woman laughing.

The laugh isn't for my benefit, however, because when I say hello she stops laughing and says very seriously, "I apologize for all the trouble Jacob is giving you."

(6)   "It's no trouble," I say. "He just wanted to use the telephone."

"Well, thank you, anyway. He was supposed to go home with a friend after school. I don't know what could have happened . . ." She speculates for a while about what might have happened. Imagines emergencies, consults her datebook, considers quarrels. I begin to tune out, just saying "Right" every now and then. She has a nice voice. I understand why she has to explain everything, but I'm having trouble listening because I'm thinking about my painting. The boy, Jacob, is thinking about it, too, walking around it and giving it an occasional nudge with his toe. To see if I really killed it, I suppose.

"What?" I say. Something on the audio track has caught my attention.

"I said I'm afraid I don't know your name."

"Celine. Celine Morienval."

"I'm Mrs. Barker. Jacob's mother. I understand that you're a friend of Mel Hollingsford."

I don't know where she got that idea.

"No. I'm just living here. My stepmother and me. We're subletting the apartment from Mr. Hollingsford."

"Oh. I see," she says. She wants to know a lot more then. How old I am, where my father is, what my stepmother does, and the name of my school. This I discover is all very reasonable on her part, because she is about to ask if Jacob can stay with me until she gets home from work.

Excellent.

"Jake," I say, holding the phone so she can hear. "Do you want to stay with me, or should your mother call Mrs. Puccio downstairs and see if you can go there? What do you want? To stay here? He wants to stay here," I report.

His mother promises to be home by five-thirty, and I think I remember to say goodbye, but I might not have, because I know all at once what I am going to write about Celine on *Test Patterns*.

I get busy right away. I have this big fat marker that makes in a single stroke a red line with gold borders. It is rather wonderful, but deadly poisonous, so I don't use it very often. Now, however, seems the time.

"But Can Celine Fly?" I write in big letters, right across the middle.

"Who's that?" asks Jake, who is watching me with great interest.

"That's me. I am Celine Morienval." I underline my name once and then begin to draw, very carefully, big drops dripping from the line. They might be tears.

"Are you a artist? My dad's a artist."

"Yes, I am an artist." I take out my special silver marker, but I'm distracted by this child and I don't know what to write next. What does Celine do? Whatever will become of her?

"Can I write something?" he asks.

"Yes. Yes, you can." I thrust the marker into his hand and gallop to the refrigerator. When in doubt, see what is in the refrigerator. There is not much. I find a long (8) cucumber wrapped in plastic. An extraordinary object. From Chile, I think.

When I get back to *Test Patterns*, Jake is hopping from foot to foot, waving the marker around.

"What should I write?" he asks, and I am disappointed in him.

"*I* can't tell you. You must make up your own mind." But then I forgive him and offer a hint. "It has to be about Celine Morienval."

He nods thoughtfully and scrunches down and starts printing very carefully in the lower left-hand corner of the painting. He has to check every now and then on the spelling of my name, even making me move at one point so that he can see. I'm very touched, but I forget about him, because I see all at once that *Test Patterns* is not a test pattern at all. It is a flight plan. A convergence of flee and fly. Everything is marked out clearly, because it is for use at night. Here is Celine Morienval, and here is the way she was meant to fly. There are dangers—electrical storms, imminent collisions, warning lights. It is all very clear. It can be made better, of course. There is so much to do.

"There," Jake says.

"What?"

"There." In very neat second-grade printing he has written: CELINE MORIENVAL HAS DIRTY FEET.

He's watching me carefully with his giggly little eyes in case I try to belt him. I don't belt him, but I'm crushed. Seen through. When I stand up, I can see that he's right. Celine Morienval has dirty feet. I kicked my sneakers off (9) as soon as I came in, and the loft floor is black with graphite and charcoal. Neither Catherine nor I are big on vacuuming.

"Feet of clay!" I cry. "Feet of clay!" I march with as much dignity as possible over *Test Patterns* or *Flight Plan* or whatever it is. I can feel the texture of the paint with my bare feet. It is extraordinary. It is like the texture of ripples fossilized in slate.

"Can I do that?"

"Of course."

Jake sits down and takes off his shoes and socks. He folds his socks up and puts them in his shoes, and then trots around the loft on his little pink feet to get them dirty. I am beginning to like this Jacob person.

"Feet of clay!" he yells and jumps on the painting. We march around for a while. He shows me the polka hop. You may think it is strange for an artist to behave this way. It is not. We all hate what we create.

I'm suddenly so bored I want to die.

"Let's watch TV," I say. Jake stops dancing around and looks at me with wild surmise.

"Do you have a TV?"

"Of course. Don't you?"

"No," he says. "My mom doesn't believe in TV."

"She must be a remarkable woman."

"A what?"

"A remarkable woman. A woman of almost super-human powers of disbelief."

"Yeah," he says. "Where is it?"

It is behind a screen at one end of the loft. My father wanted to "store it away" when we first moved in. Actually *un*plug it, but I couldn't allow that. I love TV. I watch it as much as I can. It is almost a duty, I think. You see, one day there will come a moment when everyone in the whole world will be watching television at exactly the same time. Everyone. The President and the rulers of the world. The Dalai Lama. Nomads in their tents. Eskimos. Chilean torturers and transplant surgeons. Operators of nuclear plants. Terrorists making their little bombs out of *plastique*. It is hard work. They all need a break. "Let's see what's on TV," says the Pope to Jerry Falwell.

At that moment, when we're all seated very quietly in front of the television, bathed in its comforting glow like limp little mummies, all the same soft, pale color at last—at that moment . . .

There is a mystery here. I'm not sure what will happen. Perhaps we'll all do a slow fade. The real people will be able to relax. No one will be watching anymore every move they make. Rhoda will tell Mary Tyler Moore about this guy she likes and Michael J. Fox will help his dumb sister with her homework. Everything will be better. There'll be no distractions.

"Let's watch Judge Wapner," I say and turn the set on.

"Who?"

"Judge Wapner on *The People's Court*. It's like a real court. If you have a problem, you don't take the law into your own hands. You take it to Judge Wapner."

"Yeah," says Jake. We sit down on the couch together. We are still there. We don't fade or disappear. Someone must not be watching. Someone must be out shopping or going to the bathroom. It is probably my grandmother. I used to live with her before she moved to Sun City. She watches TV sometimes, but warily, on her feet, with a book in her hand or the spoon she's been stirring the soup with. So she won't get caught.

She worried about how much television I watched when I first went to live with her. She didn't think I was making enough friends my own age. She suggested once that I "plan my viewing" and bought me a *TV Guide*, but I couldn't use it. I tried, but I felt like a fool. It's one thing to watch *Dallas* and *Dynasty*, but it's another to *plan* to watch them. I mean, when a bum goes through the dumpster behind McDonald's, he doesn't *plan* what he's going to eat. Maybe he likes it to be a surprise. I am like that bum. A sort of bag lady of television. I just like to see what I'll find.

I show Jake how to work the remote control. I don't think he's ever seen one. As a matter of fact, my grandmother's television didn't have one either, and I didn't appreciate how wonderful a remote control is. I thought they were for people with broken legs, old ladies who have these chairs that stand them up, but slowly. People in bed with the curtains open and no pajamas.

I was very wrong. A remote control opens a whole new dimension of television viewing. Without it, life is flat, dull. With it, various, new, exciting. One need never be completely bored again. Even if all the channels have boring stuff, you can zip through them, looking for that little high, or you can construct interesting dialogues by going back and forth between one program and another. It is always better.

I call the remote control my zapper. You don't want to even consider buying three rooms of carpeting for $212 (thick, bouncy foam padding and installation extra)? *Zap!* What will happen if you don't send the evangelist that you see before you four and one half million dollars? Don't you realize that he will be struck dead right before your . . . *Zap!*

Jake picks up the principles rapidly. For ten minutes we watch nothing but commercials.

"Wait! Wait!" I say. "This is my favorite." A small town somewhere in the Midwest, washed with eternal sun and pure air.

"Why do you like this one?" Jake wants to know.

"I lived there before I came here. That's my home-town." The camera, obviously a stranger, picks its way down the street, asking everyone: Where is that Burger King? They all know. In my town they all know.

> *This is a Burger King town . . .*
> *We know how burgers should be . . .*

"That's my little brother on his tricycle. Do you see? He's pointing. He's saying, 'There it is! It's that way!'"

And that's my best friend, Laura Cunningham . . . Her dad just bought her that car she's washing . . . And there're some people who just got married. Oh, look! It's Debby and Steve! What a relief! I can't tell you! Debby had mono and they thought they were going to have to postpone everything, but she looks great to me . . ."

(13)

"That isn't real!" says Jake, pushing his face into mine. "You don't really know those people!" He is scornful, but nervous about the tears in my eyes.

No. He's right. It isn't my hometown. I just made that up. But why, then, am I so happy for Debby and Steve?

I blow my nose and then we really do watch *The People's Court*. The case of the Flagrant Feline. The case of Button, Button, Who's Got the Button. I can't tell who's lying and who's telling the truth. But justice is done. Judge Wapner knows.

Jake's mother and Catherine arrive during a news special on nuclear-plant safety. They must have met outside the door, but once inside the loft, they drift apart, like boxers retiring to neutral corners.

Catherine glances at Jake and me in a faint, shocked way and wanders into the kitchen with her shopping bags. I'm not alarmed by this behavior. It is Catherine's way of saying hello. The truth is that we don't get along too well. Or perhaps it is more serious than that. Whenever I drift into view, I seem to induce in Catherine profound existential anguish. What my old friend and Godpapa Jean-Paul calls *nausea*. She watches me closely for signs of fading around the edges, indications of growing insubstantiality, the first symptoms of deconstruction. This is not, perhaps, as loony as it sounds. After all, no one told her when she was a young graduate student brushing strands of hair from her ovoid face that the French professor with whom she had fallen in love had secreted somewhere in Iowa a lumpy adolescent. I was an unlooked-for absurdity, a serpent in the bosom, a cloud before the sun, a shock, a handful, as my grandmother announced upon her sudden decision to move to Sun City, where, to her intense regret, teenagers were allowed only on closely supervised visits. There was a short, bitter custody battle between my father and my mother, and Catherine lost. My father hopes that we will grow to love one another. We must have much in common since we are so nearly the same age, he observed just before he left on an impromptu lecture tour of seven major European universities. A man of powerful imagination and boundless hope, he has been gone six weeks now.

While Catherine is unloading her bag of gourmet goodies from Marshall Field's, Jake's mother is surveying the premises and wondering if any of this could possibly be catching. Ordinarily I would arm myself with cold contempt, but she is a comely person, even wearing running shoes underneath her pin-striped suit. Jake is glad to see his mother, and while he distracts her, I shuffle the worst of the mess—*Test Patterns*—off into a corner.

"You must be Celine," says Mrs. Barker, and gives me a terrific smile which warms me up in spite of myself. "Thanks for taking care of Jacob for me. I don't know what I would have done. I had this presentation to give at the bank, and well . . ." She laughs in a helpless way which must send all the vice presidents at the bank running for a glass of water.

"That's okay. It was no trouble."

"Thank you, anyway." Her eyes wander about and then come to rest again on her son. "Jacob! Where are your shoes and socks? And look at your feet!"

Jake panics, naturally, and looks wide-eyed at me. How could I have led him astray in this way?

"We were just watching some TV . . ." I begin, trying to fix her eye with mine so that she won't ask me to look at my feet, too. I'm saved by Catherine moseying up. She's frowning in that perplexed way that means she is getting ready to come to the surface and be offensive.

"Turn that bloody thing off, Celine. A person can't think," she says. A remark which demonstrates how dismally she fails to appreciate the point of television. She stares at Mrs. Barker. "I hate American television," she says.

Mrs. Barker blinks rapidly. "We don't have a television ourselves," she says finally. "I don't know why. We just never felt the need . . ."

Catherine snorts. "Nobody in their right mind would watch that junk." Mrs. Barker hardly seems to hear. There is something else she wants to tell us. "I'm working full-time now—since Jacob's father and I have separated—and I try to make the time that Jacob and I are together special," she says quietly.

"Special?"

"Yes. It isn't how much time you spend with your child, you know. It's the quality of the time. We like to pay full attention to each other in the evening, don't we, (16) Jacob? Make every minute count." She tousles Jacob's hair and immediately smooths it out again.

Catherine has never heard anything so bizarre. "Really?" she asks. "What do you do?"

"Oh, play games, talk about our day. That sort of thing. We're building a model airplane right now. I'm actually enjoying it. I think I must have been deprived as a child."

"Why?" asks Catherine, very seriously.

"Well. You know. Only boys were supposed to build model airplanes . . ." It makes Mrs. Barker uneasy to have to explain her little joke. She doesn't realize that humor is simply a mystery to Catherine.

"Sounds a bloody bore to me," says Catherine bitterly.

Mrs. Barker looks her over coolly. She is not, I realize, without nerve of her own, and she's beginning to come to some decisions about how to deal with Catherine. "It isn't a bore," she says simply. "And there isn't anyone I would rather spend time with. Jacob? Get your shoes and socks on now. We're going home."

Jacob dodges out from under her hand and runs to the window. "Can I come over here tomorrow?" he shouts out over the city.

"Really, Jacob!" Mrs. Barker blushes. "I imagine that Celine will have things of her own to do tomorrow."

"No. It's okay with me," I say, but this answer doesn't seem to please her for some reason, and so we part, ships in the night, nothing settled.

When Jacob and his mother are out of the way, Catherine discovers *Test Patterns*.

"What's this?" she asks.

"You know. *Test Patterns*."

"I can see that. What the hell have you been doing to it?"

"Oh, this and that. Trying out some things. You know. 'We murder to create,' " I say, making airy little gestures in the air.

" 'Dissect.' "

"What?"

" 'Dissect.' 'We murder to dissect.' "

"Oh. Is that right?" She *is* right, of course. I don't know how I got mixed up about that. Murderers should keep their motives straight.

"Oh, well," says Catherine to console me. "It wasn't much good anyway."

"Yes, it was!" I bellow so suddenly we are both stunned. "And now I've ruined it!"

Catherine is surprised that anyone could care so much about a piece of canvas with paint smeared on it. "If you feel that bad, do it over."

"No! No! No! It can't be done over. It's destroyed! Lost forever!" I blubber around the loft a few more times while Catherine makes one or two other dumb suggestions before she goes off in disgust to fry some eggs.

I don't care. Blubbering absorbs my whole attention. I am one of the world's great blubberers.

"Ruined forever! My life is ruined!" I bellow again, and wobble off to bed, a great blob of melting Jell-O.

My bed is high in the air, close to the ceiling, a sort of swing *mit* futon—the fancy of Mel Hollingsford of which I am most fond. I pull up the rope ladder after me and moan a bit more, assuming the pose in which I would most like to be found dead. But my heart isn't really in my grief. I am distracted by the calendar pasted over my head, each succeeding day blotted out with Magic Marker and imagination. By swinging my legs up and resting my feet on the ceiling, I can make my bed sway gently as I contemplate my future. Three more weeks of school, and I shall burst forth like a rose in time-lapse photography. It's all arranged. A little deal worked out with my father when I arrived just after the New Year. I am going to spend the summer with my friend Sybil in a small villa in Montebene in the foothills above Florence. And—I have not confided this point to anyone yet—I am not coming back. All I have to do to ascend to this heaven is show a little maturity. My father's exact words. "Show a little maturity," he said, which I've doped out to mean: Pass all your courses, avoid detection in all crimes and misdemeanors, don't get pregnant.

He was alarmed, you see, by those reports pouring in like early returns from Iowa. Nothing had been left out. The plastic shoes melting in the dryer, the rabid pet squirrel, the two counts of obscenity (the first when I tried out for the cheerleading squad, the second for my entry in the Sons of Freedom Art Show, theme: My Family), the almost bombed courses in trigonometry and biology, and finally, of course, my unsanctioned stint as road manager for the all-girl rock band Oozing Baby in its triumphant tour throughout northwest Iowa. A story, it has been said, for which the world is not yet ready.

Show a little maturity, indeed. It has been child's play. (19) I'm not only passing all my courses but will at the end of the term have enough credits to graduate a year early. I have been as honest and forthright in my dealings with authority as my natural instincts will allow, and as for getting pregnant . . . May I quote Mrs. Barker: "We don't have a television ourselves. I don't know why. We just never felt the need."

Show a little maturity. Really, it's hard not to be offended. If I was any more mature, I'd have Alzheimer's disease. No, shortly I will be drifting over the hills of Tuscany, my box easel strapped to my back, the Mediterranean sun bronzing my brow. What could possibly go wrong?

T W O /

The next morning in English class Mr. Carruthers hands back our papers on *Catcher in the Rye*.

The first two pages of mine are decorated with the usual red scribbles. Sentence Fragments are my main problem. I find them irresistible. After that, not a word. Just a note. At the end. See Me.

Mr. Carruthers has returned to the front of the class and is busy climbing up on his desk. It is his favorite perch, next to the windowsill. He sits on one or the other, cross-legged or half reclining in a boyish pose. Sometimes he rocks back and forth as he talks, and eventually he will fall out the window. I believe this is his fate.

I wonder why he wants to see me. Does he suspect plagiarism? That doesn't seem likely. Nobody can have thought that this paper was plagiarized. I calculated this theme at about a C-plus, or even a B-minus, depending (21) on where it was in the stack and, possibly, what Mrs. Carruthers learned at the doctor's. She and Mr. Carruthers are trying to conceive a child, but have been having difficulties. He has told us all about it in considerable detail. It is very interesting.

"When did you write this?" he asks when I take the paper up after class. "In the commercial breaks of *Miami Vice?*"

I blush prettily. Or anyway I blush. It wasn't *Miami Vice*, though. It was *Soul Train* and a movie on Channel 66. I thought I had worked fairly hard, considering. There had even been a moment when I had thought the television was too distracting, and so I switched to the channel where they do nothing but sell jewelry and radar detectors at fantastic savings. Ordinarily I never watch this channel, because I knew a girl in Iowa who used to watch it all the time even though she was warned. "I never buy any of the stuff," she kept saying, but then as soon as she graduated from high school she got married and moved into a trailer, bought a dish antenna, started a doll collection and wore gold chains. "See?" said my grandmother. This is the sort of risk I'm willing to take for my education.

"Is it that bad?" I say. "I'm sorry. I'll try to do better next time."

Mr. Carruthers shakes his head and tosses the paper at me so that I have to do this little floor exercise like Nadia Comaneci to catch it. As if it is of absolutely no value whatsoever and why don't I just toss it in the wastepaper basket?

"Rewrite it," he says.

"No. That's okay. I guess I was just being lazy. I won't ask to rewrite it. It wouldn't be fair to the other kids." I think I sound pretty noble, but Mr. Carruthers just sneers at me.

"I didn't ask if you *wanted* to rewrite it. I'm *telling* you to rewrite it. Now get it out of here." He whips out his red pencil and a stack of blue books to show that the interview is over.

"What if I don't?"

Mr. Carruthers blinks at me. He is surprised, I think, that he has driven me to lippiness, but not unpleased.

"Then you fail."

"The paper?" I ask, rapidly calculating.

"The course."

"Wait a minute! Even with an F on this paper, I get a C in the course if I get a B on the final. Right?"

"Wrong. If you don't finish the assigned work, you haven't finished the course. And if you don't have a good excuse—which you don't have, as far as I can tell—you get an F."

I am about to argue some more, point out the in-alienable right of students to get Ds and Cs if that's what they want, when Mr. Carruthers sighs and starts rubbing his forehead as if I'm a migraine headache.

"What's wrong with you, Celine? You're not here to get Cs and Ds, or any grade, for that matter. You're here to do your very best, and I'm not going to be satisfied with anything else. Do you really want to just squeak by, (23) not working up to your potential? Is that really what you want?

"Look at this . . . this . . ." He gestures at the blue books, and I know what word he means, although he never says it. "Do you think I enjoy reading this stuff? I shouldn't have to read anything but the best you can do. You want me to do my best, don't you? Do you think it's fair for you to do any less?"

I don't know what to say. I'm not actually such a demanding student, but when people start asking me if I'm being fair, I immediately feel like a drug smuggler anyway, and Mr. Carruthers is sitting there telling me that he likes and cares about me and I am letting him down. This is pretty heavy stuff.

"Is there some reason you're having difficulty with this assignment? Would it do any good if we talked about it?"

He really means it, I think. This school is full of dedicated teachers. And there are reasons, but I can't tell him what they are.

Right from the start, I thought there was something queer about the assignment. It didn't seem right to have to read Catcher in the Rye in high-school English. It's about this boy who is terribly sensitive and having trouble adjusting to the world. His name is Holden Caulfield and I don't very much like him because I think he whines just a little too much, and sometimes when he says this very moving stuff I definitely have the feeling that he is congratulating himself on what a sweet, misunderstood kid he really is. (As I think of it, I realize that he would (24) probably admit I'm right, and that he is just a rotten phony like everybody else. He would feel good about admitting this for a while, and then realize that that made him a sort of phony to the second power . . . Honestly, he wears me out.) But the point I am trying to make is that it seems to me to be sort of a smash-and-grab for the high schools to start taking this book over. Because, unless we are going to start throwing up on the teacher every time he brings the subject up, we are going to have to pretend that he is really very wise and understanding and not at all like the adults in *Catcher in the Rye*. It really makes me uncomfortable for Mr. Carruthers to talk about this book, because I can tell that it means a lot to him, and that he wanted us to understand what a big difference it has made in his own life, even though he is getting a little seedy. In fact, the real reason I am having trouble with this assignment is that I can't get it out of my head that Mr. Carruthers *is* Holden Caulfield. After he recovered from his nervous breakdown, he managed to be accepted by Columbia with just a high-school equivalency because he was so brilliant. He graduated in three years, and went off to the University of Chicago and started his doctorate in English literature, and the whole world looked bright and promising. But then his little sister Phoebe became a groupie for a heavy-metal band and died of an overdose, and in his grief he married this ed-psych major from Englewood, New Jersey, and because he didn't have his thesis quite finished when his grants ran out, he took a job twelve years ago at this school. His thesis is still in a cardboard box on his desk at home . . . (25)

"I mean it," he says. "If there's some special problem, I want you to tell me." He is watching me with his sad blue eyes. The skin is beginning to bag a little bit underneath them.

"No. There's no special problem. I'll rewrite the paper."

"Good. That's what I wanted to hear."

Out in the hall, I am calm and businesslike, folding my paper up. Corners neatly aligned, tucking it safely into my chemistry book. Well, I think, this is no big deal. I have until Monday, but I will just sit right down and do it when I get home this afternoon. No time like the present and don't put off until tomorrow what you can do today and a stitch in time saves nine and don't cut off your nose to spite your face and you have to remember that what all those college boys want from a girl is one thing, as my grandmother used to say. The bell rings, and so my pathetic whimpers go unnoticed.

But still the day is not a complete disaster. At the end of art class Miss Denver announces that for our last and final project we are all to make portraits. There are the usual signs of distress. Sighs and whispers. Cries and moans.

"Oh, Miss Denver, I can't do people!"

"Does it have to be someone we know, Miss Denver? Does it have to?"

"Does it have to look like them, Miss Denver?"

"Oh, Miss Denver, I can't draw people. Can it be a dog? Can I make a portrait of my dog?"

Everything is made clear. It doesn't have to be someone you know. You can use photographs to work from. It would be nice if you thought about making the picture look like its subject, but the important thing is to make a *statement*. It might even be an abstract *statement*. And if you really care that much about your dog . . .

"Oh, Miss Denver, can it be my goldfish? Or somebody who's dead? What if you don't know what they look like? Can it be a *dead* goldfish?"

When Miss Denver has watered down the assignment enough so that everyone understands that they can paint or draw whatever they usually paint or draw as long as they call it a *statement*, people quiet down and start gathering up their junk. It is the last period of the day, and everyone is anxious to escape.

I am not part of this, you understand. By sliding down in my chair, I find that I can straighten out completely without standing up. My body is supported by my neck on the back of the chair, and I am paralyzed with delight. Painting a portrait! This is what I'd been dying to do, but I hadn't known how to arrange it, and now Miss Denver had made it an assignment! I know exactly whose picture I am going to paint.

Lucile Higgenbottom is the most beautiful creature on

earth. Eyes like great marbles insecurely held in their sockets, cunning joints, hair which she has dyed to the color of brass pot-scrubbers. She flirts with anorexia nervosa; her teeth are long and white. It is only a matter of weeks, maybe minutes, before some foraging TV talent scout descends on the school and carries Lucile away, trailing miles of coaxial cable and dribbling cash from his pockets.

No one apparently realizes this. Not even Lucile Higgenbottom, who is under the impression that as soon as she graduates she is going to train in word processing, save enough money to buy a house in Glen Ellyn, marry Philip Halsted, have seven children named Darell, Donna, Denise and Dennis (twins), Derek, Di, and Desdemona. I don't get it myself. If I had my life planned out that clearly, I think I would just shoot myself to save the bother of going through it. It doesn't matter. Lucile will be saved by her talent scout.

Anyway, I am as happy as Doctor Strangelove with the way my schemes are beginning to work out, and as soon as the bell rings I make a dash for Lucile.

Unfortunately, I am ambushed by Dermot Forbisher, who has been lying in wait just outside the door.

"Hi, Celine," he says, grinning like I am a Twinkie and he is going to take a bite.

"Oh. Hi, Dermot." Lucile and Philip are disappearing down the hall. Well. I'll talk to her later, unless the TV scout arrives first. Now I have to talk to Dermot.

Dermot is my . . . what is that word? It begins with

"b." Burp? *Bête noire?* Basketball? Bronchial spasm? No, boyfriend, I think. I'm not exactly sure how this happened. It certainly had nothing to do with me. I acquired him, there, on the end of my hand. Like a growth. I can imagine the doctor examining my fingers and saying, "I'm sorry Celine, but I'm afraid you have a very bad case of boyfriend." What? Me? A boyfriend? But I never ever! I must have caught it off a toilet seat.

It all began when Dermot sent me a valentine card and a two-pound box of Frango mints. I won't describe the card in any detail. It was one of those the druggist puts up high so that little kids won't drool their M&M's all over them. You know. Soft-focus tacky. I thought the only people who bought them were people who had been married for forty years and want to rekindle the flames of their love. I was upset, to tell the truth. I would as soon walk by the peep joints on Rush Street at midnight as get a card like this. And who is this Dermot, anyway? And what kind of stuff is he thinking about me?

I ask myself: What shall I do? What is the *mature* thing to do? I ponder for a while and finally decide that I will return the card with a note. I will write: "I'm afraid you have sent this card to the wrong person. Yours sincerely, Celine Morienval." And this is what I should have done. Unfortunately, while I am coming to this decision, I eat the Frango mints. Two pounds. This creates a problem, you understand. What am I supposed to do now? Shall I write: "I'm afraid you have sent this card to the wrong person. (But you have sent the Frango mints to the right person.) Yours sincerely," etc., etc.?

Of course, what I do is nothing. I throw the card in the trash after cutting out my name with nail clippers so that the garbageman won't get ideas, wipe the chocolate off my mouth, go back to school, and try to pretend the whole business was lost in the mail.

I am not going to get away with this. President Reagan or Adolf Eichmann might. But I am not. First of all, Maureen Norbert and Tiffany Mortorelli corner me in the cafeteria and want to know what am I? Stuck up or something? These two have apparently decided to be the cupids of Dermot Forbisher's great love. They tell me how much Dermot has spent on that really gorgeous card and the Frango mints, and I don't even have the decency to say thanks. I could at least be *polite*, you know. What's more, Dermot is a "hunk." Visions of cheese, raw meat, salami, blubber stripped from living whales, dance before my eyes. Hunks.

Then Dermot, after glowering at *me* in chemistry while Mr. Gordon bawls *him* out for not having learned the periodic table, follows me out into the parking lot and wants to know what am I? Frigid or something? *"You know what your problem is, Celine? You're afraid of love."*

Dermot, I have realized as I have matured, is one of those people whom love turns into a bully. Because he has this great passion for me, I am unreasonable and selfish if I don't act as if I love him. Since I'm always ready to believe anyone who tells me I'm unreasonable and selfish, I am already trapped by the time I realize I should have pushed him under a truck or something the first time I saw him. As it is, it looks as if I will have to spend the rest of my life being sensitive to Dermot's great needs and having these really tedious conversations about how difficult life is. I manage to hold him off a little by pretending that, although I love him dearly, I have this stepmother whose sole pleasure in life is nipping the passions of youth in the bud.

For the past week, Dermot has been satisfied with a few soulful looks and self-pity, but I can tell he's getting restless.

So "Hi, Celine," he says.

"Hi, Dermot."

"God, you look great!" Meaningful looks.

"Oh, Dermot. You mustn't talk that way." My passionate nature is stirred.

"I can't help how I feel!" Significant pause. "You want to go down to Wendy's and get something to eat?"

"Oh, Dermot. You know I can't. I have to go home right after school. My stepmother's practically standing there with a stopwatch." I feel some twinges of honest guilt when I trash Catherine's reputation this way. The next time we are snarling at one another over the last cream puff in the box, I will really have to give in gracefully.

Dermot shakes his head. How much can a man stand? "Sometimes I think we'll never get to really know each other. You know what I mean? If only we could spend some time together. Away from this awful place. Alone."

"Oh, I know, Dermot. But it's so difficult."

"There's this school party next Thursday night.

Couldn't we go to that together? There'll be chaperones and all."

"I'm afraid to ask. My stepmother is so impossible. I mean, she'll think I want to go to a motel or something. (31) Besides, I have to take her to Mass on Thursday night." This is risky. Does anyone have Mass on Thursday nights? Would Dermot know?

"Damn it!" Dermot savages a locker.

"Please, Dermot."

"There's someone else, isn't there." A voice from the grave.

"You know that isn't true, Dermot." I am beginning to rush my lines a little. I'm afraid that Lucile is going to leave school before I can ask her to sit for me. Dermot doesn't seem to notice. His eyes narrow, like Clint Eastwood's before he starts flapping his serape.

"I don't know what I would do if there was someone else," he says. Very quietly. With malice toward all.

"Please, Dermot. Believe me. There's no one else. Look. I'll talk to my stepmother about it. I'll ask her. Maybe she'll understand."

"Golly, Celine. If only I could meet her. Why can't I meet her? Why don't I walk you home? She'll see I'm not some kind of monster." Dermot ducks his head modestly. Shucks. Nobody with ovaries could think that *he* was a monster.

"You can't do that, Dermot. She . . . she doesn't speak English. Just French. She'll probably call the police or something if I show up with a boy."

"How can she call the police if she doesn't speak English?" Dermot wants to know. This sudden display of mental acuity disconcerts me. What do I say? She'll call the *French* police? Somehow I escape, mainly because Dermot does not actually want to walk me home. He wants to go to the gym and push hunks of metal around in hopes that they will impart even more of their hunkiness to him.

Off I trot, nose to the ground, anxious to catch up with Lucile before she escapes.

"Walk, Celine!" shouts Mr. Ferrelli outside the detention room, where he is marshaling the daily quota of fistfights and drug overdoses. They are sprawled about on benches in various postures of barely controlled violence and bliss. The benches are a gift of the class of '68.

Yes, yes, yes. I down-shift into a ground-consuming race walk, elbows working in the prescribed fashion. Past the cafeteria and the trophy case with its newly installed steel mesh, and out into the school yard, where I finally run Lucile down.

She is watching Philip perform stately maneuvers on his skateboard. Her homework—a separate notebook for each subject, divided into obscure classifications with Day-Glo tabs—cushioned against her chest, weight poised over one elegant foot encased in a white Hi-Top with four pairs of clean, multicolored laces, spine neatly curved and humming with grace. A picture no artist could paint, as my grandmother would say.

" 'lo, Lucile."

"Hi, Celine."

"Whose portrait are you going to paint for Miss Denver's class?" I ask, getting down to business.

"Martin Luther King." Lucile is thought by some to be the best painter in the whole school. She works exclusively from photographs found in *Seventeen* and *People*, and every picture is exactly alike. It is a remarkable achievement, I believe. I call her style minimal expressionism and suggested that she should reproduce an entire *People* magazine from cover to cover. It would be a knockout. "How does she do it?" critics would exclaim. "It is all there. Every detail. And yet . . . and yet . . . *completely drained of content!*" She wasn't interested, of course. If she had been interested, she couldn't have done it. Such is life.

"Who are you going to paint?" Lucile asks. Finally. Philip has run afoul of one of the cracks in the pavement, and Lucile must look away.

"You. I thought I'd make a portrait of you. Okay?"

"I already gave a picture to Philip. He's going to paint my portrait." She means she gave Philip a photograph.

"So? You're not going to get used up or anything if I make your picture, too. Anyway, I want to paint you, not a picture."

Lucile is puzzled, and then she giggles. I see that I have been deliberately misunderstood.

"I mean, I want to paint a picture of you, not a picture of a picture of you."

We both meditate on this distinction for a minute. For some reason it sounds revolutionary.

"I don't get it. Don't you want to make a picture of Dermot?"

Dermot? Who's Dermot?

"Oh, yeah, sure. But my stepmother would never let him in the house. You see, I thought you could come over to my place after school and I could make your portrait. It wouldn't take long. You could watch TV or something."

"Yeah. Your stepmother's real strict, isn't she?"

"Yeah, but what do you think?"

"My mom is, too. Are you going to the party?"

"What party?"

"The party Thursday night. Dermot said he was going to ask you."

"He did, but I don't think I can go. Anyway, what about posing for me? Do you think you could?"

"My mom won't let me go, either. Not with Philip, anyway. I mean, she'd probably let me go with a girl or something."

Slowly, like rain percolating through the topsoil and into a huge subterranean aquifer, the drift of this conversation begins to penetrate my consciousness.

"Your mom doesn't like Philip?"

Lucile shakes her head, baffled. "She doesn't trust him. Maybe it's because he can't control himself." She smiles dreamily.

A gust of wind swirls across the yard, driving rainbow-colored lottery tickets in front of it.

"What if you and I went together?" I say.

"Hey! That's an idea. We could go together." We might even run into something. Bounce off hunks. "I'll ask my mom. I've got to go now. I've got to be home at three forty-five."

"What about the portrait?" I call after her.

"I'll ask. I'll ask about that, too!"

When she is gone, I watch Philip and the other skateboarders cruise around the parking lot on their little wheels. Deft as dolphins. Serene as sharks.

No sooner am I through the door and in the refrigerator than the phone rings.

"Can I come over?" I have the feeling that I am being watched.

"Who is this?"

"Jacob. Jacob Barker."

"I don't know, Jake. I'm kind of busy right now."

"What are you doing?"

"I'm eating a green pepper and talking on the telephone."

"Are you watching TV?" Are you smoking in there? Do you have both feet on the floor?

"Yeah, but I'm doing other things, too."

"Can I come over?"

"I don't know, Jake. I'm kind of busy right now."

"I won't bother you. What are you doing?"

"Well, I've got to stretch this canvas and write this paper."

"Oh. Can I come over, anyway?"

"I don't know, Jake. I'm really kind of busy . . ." Wait a minute. Haven't I said this before? I seem to be caught in a tape loop. Doomed to say the same thing over and over. "Okay, Jake," I say. "Ask your mother."

"I can't. She's not here."

"She's not? Are you alone, Jake?"

"No. I'm with Mrs. Puccio."

"Well, ask Mrs. Puccio."

"She's asleep."

"Ask her, anyway."

"Okay."

Bang! Bang! Bang! He is pounding on the door before I can hang up.

"Goodbye, Jake," I say, opening the door.

"Wha'?" He gives me one of the looks that creamed spinach collects in the cafeteria line, as he trots by on his way to the television.

"Goodbye, Jake. That was my next line. Just after you say 'Okay' and before you say 'Goodbye, Celine. Thank you very much for inviting me over.' "

"You're kind of crazy." He adjusts the volume on the television up a few decibels.

What can I say. He *knows*. You know what's the matter with you, Celine? You're *afraid* of love.

Actually, Jake and I get along very well together. I want to stretch a canvas for my portrait of Lucile Higgenbottom, and he is too busy with the zapper for idle conversation.

I am the only person in my art class who stretches

canvases to paint on. Everyone else uses Masonite, gessoed paper, or those warpy cardboard things. I explain that I enjoy the sensuous give of the canvas beneath my brush when it is stretched within a frame, but that is not the real reason. Stretching canvas is one of the few things you can do in painting where you don't feel as if you're risking your soul, and it lets you put off actually beginning for a while. Getting started is hard for me for some reason. The first few strokes on a new canvas are very painful. It is beginning without a hope of success. It is like painting acid on my skin.

So I am busy and content. As content as a person who has surrendered control of her zapper to someone else can be. When the canvas is stretched and shrinking with its first coat of gesso, I get out the peanut butter, grab a couple of bananas, and join Jake on the couch.

"What are we watching?" I ask.

Divorce Court. Not one of my favorites. The cases are based on reality, and so the actors are insecure and ill at ease. "What can I do with material like this?" they all seem to be thinking. I try to get the zapper away from Jake, but I am hampered because I have been spreading peanut butter on my banana with my fingers.

"Don't," says Jake, holding the zapper out of reach of my clean hand. "I want to watch this."

"Why?"

"I want to see why they're getting a divorce."

"Isn't it obvious? The man wears clip-on bow ties and his wife nibbles on Sweetarts. That's grounds for divorce in California. Come on. Let's watch something else."

"Those aren't the reasons!" says Jake, very fierce.

I remember then that Jake's mother and father are

separated, and so I shut up. He wants to know why people get divorced? Perfectly reasonable. Television is the great educator.

After a few minutes I begin to have doubts. This lady wants a divorce because her husband has been having a homosexual affair and has left a disgusting device on the bathroom shelf. Her husband denies the whole thing, claiming that her charges are fabrications meant to justify an affair of her own.

"You know, Jake," I begin, very tactfully, "people get divorced for all sorts of reasons . . ." I know this is so. My mother left my father because he kept correcting her French accent. She said it was like an echo. They were living in Paris, where he was born, and every time she said anything, she'd hear this other voice saying *exactly the same thing*, just after her. At first she thought there was something wrong with her ears, because she was getting this constant feedback in her audio system, but she went to a doctor and he helped her spot the problem. Unfortunately, the only solution was radical surgery. It was necessary to take the echo right out of her life.

"What do you mean? What sort of reasons?"

"Well, I mean sometimes people get divorced not because they're kinky or anything, but just because they're incompatible. They may even love each other. They just find that their lives are going in different directions . . .

and there's this strain . . . you know, like when you stretch a piece of gum and it gets thinner and thinner . . ." What am I talking about?

"That's dumb," says Jake.

"Yes. You're right. That's dumb. But like your mom and dad . . ."

"They're not getting a divorce! They're just *sep-par-a-ted!*" He doesn't know whether to bite me or his banana.

Separated. Not divorced. Excellent. At this point Jake starts zapping the TV so fast that even Carol Burnett in a rerun can't get a word in before she disappears, and I withdraw to put a second coat of gesso on my canvas. It isn't really dry yet, but, as I have said, I am tactful.

Later we watch another news special on nuclear-plant safety. Today the issue centers on operators having to pee in a bottle, and whether it is right and in what circumstances is it okay to ask someone to pee in a bottle. One person is very upset because *trust* seems to have gone out of American life. I sneak a look at Jake to see if any of this loose talk about peeing in a bottle and *trust* is corrupting him, but I think he is falling asleep.

His eyes open wide when we hear his mother yelling "Jacob!" outside the door. There is a flurry of footsteps down the hall and the stairs. "Jacob!" she calls again, fainter but more desperate.

"Jake," I say. "Does Mrs. Puccio know where you are?"

He shrugs. All innocence. What do I think he is—a mind reader or something?

"Jake. I told you to ask Mrs. Puccio if you could come over."

He looks at me as if I had accused him of trading arms (40) for hostages. "I did! I did ask her!"

"Well, what did she say?"

"Nothing. She was asleep. I already *told* you that."

That's right, you know. He did. For some reason, I just forgot.

THREE /

The next morning is Saturday and I wake up thinking about my paper on Holden Caulfield, just like that. How fortunate that this obligation should occur to me so early in the morning, when I'm fresh and alert. I have the whole day, two days. I'll fill them up with Holden. I picture myself sitting down on the couch, a fresh pad of paper on my lap, a handful of sharpened pencils in easy reach, my rejected paper held down on the coffee table by my copy of *Catcher in the Rye*. Yes, indeed. Two whole days to devote to the revision of my paper . . . I picture myself leaping from the roof with a heartbreaking wail of despair. "Well," says the policeman, rising from an examination of my broken body, holding the note he has found with trembling hands. "It's as I thought. American literature has claimed another victim."

(42)   Why can't I write this stupid paper? I don't know. Why do I ask? I don't know that, either. I am mired forever in ignorance.

I console myself with cartoons and Froot Loops. Froot Loops are color-fast. The oranges and yellows do not leach into the milk. I wonder if this was a marketing decision; if men in three-piece suits sat around a rosewood table and stared thoughtfully into petri dishes of cereal. How would a child feel if she saw her milk turning yellow? These decisions are so difficult. It is so difficult to get into the mind of a child. They are not reliable. They will tell you anything. Staring at you with their cute little eyes, trying to figure out what you want to hear.

This meditation upon breakfast cereal is interrupted by the telephone, and I slosh milk on the floor, trying to reach it before Catherine wakes up. She needs her sleep. We both need her sleep.

"Celine?"

"Yeah. Hi, Jake. What do you want?"

He doesn't answer right away beyond saying "Uh" a couple of times. He is arranging his mental notecards.

"Uh . . . Celine?"

"Yeah?"

"Do you want to come with me?"

"I don't know. Where are you going?"

"I'm going to visit my grandmother. She lives on the farm in Indiana. Dad said I could invite anybody."

"You're going with your dad?"

"Yeah. We'll be back by ten."

"Well . . ." I am tempted. It would mean putting off working on my paper until tomorrow, but how long can (43) it possibly take, anyway? And I really should meet Jake's dad. He is an artist, after all.

"I asked Jimmy Fisher," Jake says, to help me make up my mind. "But he's going to Great America."

What more do I need to know? "Okay. When are we going?"

"When my dad gets here to pick us up. Can I come over until then?"

I don't have to answer this because I hear Jacob's mother vetoing the suggestion in the background. I'm not sure she considers me a good influence. She seemed a little, I don't know, *frosty* when we ran her down the afternoon before. She was in the dumpster out in back, searching for her only son. You would think she would be relieved to find he wasn't there, and I suppose she was, but somehow it hadn't made her truly happy.

I believe Jacob's father is surprised when the little friend who is going with them on a visit to Grandmother turns out to be me. He is polite, but appalled. As we drive south along Lake Shore Drive, we sneak little looks at one another; when our eyes happen to meet, he gives a jump and renews his grip on the wheel. He has a friendly, lumpy face. Not handsome exactly, but nice. The sort of face your grandmother would pick out in the yearbook and say, "Now, *that's* a nice-looking boy." I don't hold this against him, but neither of us can think of anything to say. Jake is no help at all, because he is busy in the backseat eating a box of Dunkin' Donuts and studying a joke book. His father tells him to give me a doughnut, and I say "Thank you" and he says "You're welcome," and there we are stuck. I can't talk about how good the doughnut is. How fresh.

I turn and watch the scenery go by. Hyde Park. The Museum of Science and Industry. I fake a pose in case he is looking—that of a young, self-confident girl not given to idle chitchat, a still center in a world going mad. A slight, mysterious smile plays about her mouth . . . No, that's not working. I feel as if I've developed a third lip.

"Can you drive?" he asks suddenly. We are on the Skyway, rising steadily on the approach to the bridge spanning the Calumet River.

"Well, sort of. I mean, I don't have a license or anything, but I did take drivers' ed. In Iowa." I warm to the topic because at last I have something to talk about. Why didn't I think of this before? "They had these crazy simulators, you know? Everybody's got a steering wheel and a brake and stuff and they show this movie up in front of the class. You're going down the street and here comes a dog making a left turn, if you know what I mean . . ."

"Great," he says. "Take the wheel."

"What?"

He doesn't answer, but it's already plain what he

means. He has let go the steering wheel and is fumbling with the camera that he has hanging around his neck. I somehow get hold of the steering wheel and we proceed over the bridge in sweeping gentle swoops. I am waiting (45) for the sound of screeching tires, the crash of metal. My vision blurs, but I am unable to blink. I hear him clicking away with his camera.

What I had been going to tell him was that the amazing thing about these simulators was that nothing you did—slamming the brakes on, turning the steering wheel—nothing had any effect on the movie. So I told the basketball coach, who also taught drivers' ed, that this seemed to me not to be a very good lesson, since students might get the idea that nothing they might do mattered, and he said, "We don't need any more advice from you, Morienval," and in revenge he made me stay on the simulators forever, even when the other kids got to go in a real car.

"You can let go now."

"What?"

"You can let go the wheel now. I just wanted to get some pictures of those black towers. I think they're for lifting some bridge. They've always fascinated me. The trouble is, you can't stop your car here . . . You can let go now, I said."

"What?"

"Let go of the steering wheel! I can't drive unless you let go!"

"What?"

"Are we all going to die?" calls Jake with mild interest from the backseat.

"No, no," says his father, prying my fingers loose one

by one. "You have very strong hands," he says.

"Thank you," I say.

"You're a painter, aren't you? Jacob said you were."

"Yes."

"Good. An artist has to have strong hands." As a reward Jake presses another doughnut into my strong artist hand and I cram the whole thing into my mouth.

Mr. Barker is amused. By my capacity, perhaps. "Good?" he says.

"Mmmpf," say I. There is nothing like a close brush with death to stimulate the appetite.

For the rest of the trip we talk about art. Not beauty and truth and all you need to know, but about the *stuff* of art. Paint, paper, charcoal . . . the varieties of India ink. Pelikan is thin, grayish. It tends to bloom, tinting any wash laid over it. The Pelikan sepia blooms as well, but it is lovely stuff. If you add a bit of black, you get a color close to that of the ink that Rembrandt used. His inks were made of gall, Mr. Barker tells me. To think about it makes my mouth water at the imagined acidity.

This is what real artists talk about, I think. Not Significance. Not Form. We are enamored of small things. The velvety smear of vine charcoal, the smell of linseed oil, the ghostly grays left behind by a kneadable eraser. Some things work. Some things don't. We are careful not to say more. The mysteries must be respected. For some reason I can't take my eyes off Mr. Barker's hands.

The fingers are long and spatulate. Clean little black hairs curl on his knuckles. I feel my throat contract at the notice of them.

"What did the irresistible force say to the immovaba-ba-bable object!" Jake bellows from behind me.

"Eeek!" I say, the word squeezed out of me by Mr. Barker's hands, really, but Jake hits me over the head with his joke book anyway.

Jacob's grandmother's house sits all alone on top of a hill. There is not a tree, not a shrub anywhere. The lawn is cut short right up to the foundation.

As we pile out of the car, an old woman comes out to the porch and waves us away.

"It's me, Mom. Paul!" says Mr. Barker. She is not satisfied. She totters down the stoop and across the pathless expanse of grass, still fluttering her hands. The wind tugs at her brown-and-yellow housecoat and she must watch her step, but she watches us, too, saving her voice until she is close.

"I don't want her here," she says fretfully to Mr. Barker. She picks up the hem of her housecoat and shakes it at me. "Shoo!" she says. "Shoo!"

"This is Celine, Mom," Mr. Barker says in a loud, patient voice. "She's a friend of Jacob's."

The old woman drops the housecoat and arches her back to stare up in her son's face. Her neck is long and sinewy. "I know who she is," she says abruptly.

Mr. Barker nods and smiles uneasily. "Celine. Jacob's friend, Celine."

The old woman gathers Jacob protectively under her brown-and-yellow wing. "Come with me, Jacob," she says. "You must be starved. They didn't give you any (48) lunch, did they? No, of course not."

A table is set on the porch, despite the cold wind. For lunch there are bologna sandwiches with yellow mustard on white bread with the crusts cut off, dry curls of carrots, small plastic containers of applesauce with the foil lids turned back, a Hostess cupcake cut in quarters, flowered paper cups of lime Kool-Aid that blow away out to the surrounding cornfields when they are empty.

Jacob nibbles his sandwich into the form of a car and drives it over my plate and into my lap.

"I will bite your wheels off," I whisper.

"I could get Mrs. Drover to come in every morning, Mom," Mr. Barker is saying. "It would really be best, I think."

"Drover? No! Don't want her. Talks my ear off. Never understands how I want things done."

"But, Mom, you can't really manage . . ."

"I manage!" says the old woman, and glares at me in triumph.

"I'll bite your head off," I whisper in Jacob's ear, and her hen's eyes cloud with fear because she can't hear me.

We may be enemies for life, but because we are both women we must clear the table. We huddle over the blackened sink, brewing instant coffee with hot tap water.

"You are a good girl," she says, not meaning a word. "Not like the other one. She wants to put me away. You won't put me away in that home, will you?" She touches my sleeve with dry fingers.

I consider: the windowsill crowded with withered squash, a crocheted bag of rubber bands hanging from a (49) hook, the stack of *Farm Journals* resting on the open oven door.

"You must let Mrs. Drover come. Every day."

"Oh, I won't have that. No, don't think for a moment . . ." She leans close. "She isn't clean."

"Still . . ." I am firm. I measure the coffee exactly. Pour in the water. As the flavor bursts, she surrenders. "Oh, you are old for such a long time!" She frets over the sugar bowl in the center of a tin tray. "You think it won't happen to you, but it will. You may live a long time, but most of life is old, old, old!"

After lunch Jake and I follow his father out to the barn, where he is tearing out a row of milking stalls. They were built to last forever; coated with ancient dung and cow hair, the gray wood warps against great square nails. Mr. Barker explains that the farmer who rents the fields needs the space to store his corn picker. I offer to help as I watch him pull on a pair of work gloves. The leather is blackened, creased, and supple.

"Thanks," says Mr. Barker. "Maybe you could take Jacob on a walk or something. That would be a big help."

This is not what I had in mind, but I accede gracefully and let Jake drag me away to a creek at the back of the forty acres.

The stream is in a deep gully, felted with the brown leaves of the past year. They clog the waterfalls, staining the pools the color of tea. We gather branches and stones (50) and build a dam. It is difficult. We have to take off our shoes and socks; our feet and hands are freezing. At first Jacob is very much in charge. He gives me orders. He knows how things are to be done. Suddenly he begins to cry because his hands are so cold. I hold him on my lap and put his hands under my sweatshirt to warm them.

"I like your dad," I say. He isn't interested. Why shouldn't I like his dad?

"I like your mom, too."

"Do you like my grandmother?" He squints up at me slyly. A test question.

"No. Do you?"

"No. She's so old. Do you like the President?"

"No. He's old, too. Do you like Barbie dolls?"

"No!" Jake hoots. "Do you like elephants?"

"Yes. Do you?"

"Yes. Little ones. Listen:

"I went to the animal fair.
   The birds and the beasts were there.
   The old baboon by the light of the moon
   Was combing his all-burnt hair."

he sings in a high sweet voice.

"Auburn," I say.

"What?"

"Auburn. Not all-burnt."

"What's that?"

"It's a color—sort of red, I think."

"Oh. I thought it was burnt black. Sort of like yours."

"Oh. Do you like my hair?"

"No. I think it's awful hair. Do you like my hair?"

"No. I think it is the awfulest hair I ever saw." I sigh. This must be why we get along so well. We agree on so many things.

When Jake's hands are warm again, we abandon our dam to the forces of nature and explore the creek downstream. We move silently, keeping our heads down so that we won't be seen. A war party, creeping up on the isolated homestead, slaughter and rapine in our minds. Revenge. Revenge for the plow, the barbed-wire fence, smallpox and the slaughtered buffalo, the nuclear plants built over faults in the earth and the exhausted water table, the rain like vinegar and the tattered ozone.

The creek tumbles down a broken ledge of limestone into a clear pool. An old beech leans over it, a broken tree house falling slowly through its branches. A thick, knotted rope dangles down. Jake and I swing together out over the still water. The skin on my chapped hands cracks, I hold so tight.

"Hey, you two. Be careful. That rope is old," Mr. Barker calls, coming to fetch us away. "Go say goodbye to your grandmother, Jacob," he says when we tumble down at his feet together.

He helps me up, forgets to drop my hand, and keeps

me there by the old beech as Jake sweeps away, arms outstretched and roaring like a jet.

"I should have warned you about my mother," Mr. Barker says. "She's slipping a bit. Still strong, but she gets confused . . ."

(52)

"That's okay," I say. I feel my mind has flitted out of my skull like a swallow. It sits across the pool in the bare branches there, watching us stand together, hands linked.

"Yes, I knew you would understand, but I thought I should say something."

I move my thumb slightly, testing the feel of his skin. He starts; I catch a glimpse of our reflection in the dark water as he throws my hand away.

"I put this rope up," he says. He grasps it high over his head and tries to pull himself up. The rope creaks, and he lets go. "A long time ago, that was," he says. He looks shocked. "A *long* time ago."

He makes a wild, pointless gesture at the tree. "I used to come down here and draw. When I was supposed to be doing chores, you know. I used to feel guilty as hell, because my dad would get absolutely furious. He called it wasting time, and he couldn't stand that. People who wasted time starved to death or drank themselves to death or simply went out of their heads. I believed it, too, but I couldn't help myself. I was wild to draw then."

"Up in the air. In the tree house."

He smiles at me. "Yes. Up in the air. My first studio."

"Do you have a studio now?"

"Oh, yes. Not as nice, though." He studies my sneakers, my all-burnt hair. "You want to come see it sometime?"

"Yes."

"You'd be disappointed, I'm afraid. It's not as nice as (53) this one."

It is beginning to grow dark as we climb up from the creek toward the house. Mr. Barker keeps his distance, hunched over in thought as he walks, his hands in his pockets. Jake circles back, still running. He clips my elbow as he roars past, not hard, but I feel so brittle that I am afraid something has broken.

The lawn is already wet with dew. I can feel the clean moisture seeping into my sneakers. I bend over and sweep the grass with my fingers.

"It's wet," I say, and hold out my hand to Mr. Barker. He takes my fingers in his for a moment more but says nothing at all. What are you doing, I ask myself, careful not to answer.

"Where are we going to eat?" Jake calls, coming to earth again. "Are we going to eat here?"

"No. Not here," his father says. "Somewhere. We'll stop somewhere. You can pick it out."

"Taco Bell?"

"If we find one."

"All right!" Jake runs up the porch steps, leaps into the air to slap at some wind chimes hanging over his head. The sound is sharp and pointed like broken glass.

Because my feet are wet, because the old woman and I are confused about who I really am, I stay on the porch as Jake and his father say goodbye. I watch through the screen door. It is cloudy with cobwebs and the skeletons of long-dead mayflies.

"You're not staying for supper?" says Jacob's grandmother. She is sitting in an old armchair in front of the television, the molded tray of a TV dinner balanced on her knees.

"No. Not this time. I've got to get Jacob home. Jean will be upset if we're too late."

His mother nods, and leans forward so that she can peer at me around the dark bulk of his legs. I don't believe that she can see me through the dark screen from the lighted room, but her eyes are hard, bright, and focused.

On the way home, we all sit together in the front seat of the Toyota. Jake twists in the seat belt we are sharing, so he can see out the window. When we approach a small town, he picks out the Golden Arches, the Taco Bells, the pale Colonel.

"What do you guys want?" Mr. Barker says. "Make up your minds."

We squirm with indecision, but Jake finally decides on McDonald's. He insists we use the drive-thru so he can talk into the speaker. He leans over me to shout out his father's window, his face pale and tense with responsibility.

As we drive away, the car is warm and steamy with the smell of french fries and quarter-pounders. Our Cokes are secure, sealed with lids that make a stretched pop as I push the straws through them. This is the plan of junk food: we are to drive forever through the night, clear across the country, never leaving our car, until we're finally stopped by the sea. We will arrive just as the sun is rising, and Mr. Barker and I will walk hand in hand down the beach as Jacob runs ahead to frolic in the azure waves. We will never have a moment's worry, because our lost credit cards will be replaced anywhere in the world at a day's notice (some restrictions may apply).

When we are finished eating, I gather the empty wrappers together and stuff them into a paper bag by my feet. Jake leans his head against my shoulder and reads road signs. This means stop. This means yield. This means merge . . . Abruptly he falls asleep, and his father and I begin to talk in soft voices. He tells me of his worries about his mother. He wonders how much longer she can be allowed to live alone on the farm. Because of a falling water table, a new well needs to be dug or the house hooked into the municipal system. Either would be expensive, and what would be the point if the farm has to be sold? He feels guilty because this worry about money has somehow infected the decisions about his mother's future. I am glad that he talks about such things to me. I try to reflect. Show maturity. I seem to say the right things. Jacob is glowing away beside me like a miniature space heater, and I watch the dark landscape flow by outside in perfect contentment.

"Is Jacob asleep?" asks Mr. Barker. "Excuse me." He leans across and makes some adjustment to our seat belt. As he sits back, I feel his hand fall on my leg. I stiffen and my eyes lock on the distant orange glow of the city as Mr. Barker begins to speak again in the same soft voice. Now he is telling me about the dangers of working on a farm. Of arms lost in corn pickers, tractors toppling, the mysterious gases generated by silage, the secret malevolence of the cow. I am almost in a trance, thinking about the hand. It doesn't move. The fingers are curled quietly and happily over my kneecap.

I wonder if it is simply one of those little accidents. Someone squeezing behind your seat at the movies brushes your hair or, falling in a bus, catches your shoulder . . . Not always accidental, of course, these little accidents. Even I know that. But we can pretend. I'll simply recite some little story of my own, clear my throat, and brush the hand away. "Oh! Excuse me," Mr. Barker will say. "I thought you were the gearshift." We will both have to chuckle.

"My cousin was almost electrocuted by a milking machine," I say bravely. Nothing else happens. *My* hand, the hand that is supposed to do the brushing, remains where it is, hanging limply over the back of the seat. It is amused at the little flurry of electrical activity at the top of my brain stem. You think you're still in charge? it seems to say. Didn't you know that there are moments when the body makes its own decisions?

Yes, I know. I always knew. The sentry's head nods and his eyes close as the enemy creeps close through the fog and rain. The drowning man stretches out his arms on the ocean floor and inhales . . .

"The system probably wasn't grounded properly," says Mr. Barker. "Farmers try to install this modern stuff on their own. To save money. But it really isn't safe."

"Oh, no. You've got to be careful. Storing fuel. That's another thing. The pressure builds and builds. You don't know what to do. You feel like you're going to explode."

"Hmm? Oh, yeah . . ." Mr. Barker decides to change the subject for some reason. "I hope you had a nice time today," he says. "I felt a bit guilty about . . . well, I just hope you had a nice time."

A nice time. Plain, lame little words, to describe a critical moment in my life. I begin to roll my eyes in his direction. They move reluctantly in their sockets. "It was . . ." I have to stop and swallow. "It was one of the nicest days I ever had," I say. He glances at me, startled, and tightens his grip on the steering wheel. With both hands. I look down and see in the dim light of a passing billboard that one of his work gloves has fallen off the dashboard and onto my knee. It must have happened when he was messing with the seat belt.

"I mean, since I came to live here in Chicago," I say quickly, trying to take everything back. "Or since last Saturday. I had a really nice time last Saturday."

"Oh?" says Mr. Barker, puzzled but distinctly relieved. "What did you do?"

What did I do? I went to the Laundromat, I remember that very clearly. "Various . . . various things," I say, and lapse into miserable silence. Mr. Barker doesn't say anything, either. He hunches over the wheel, brooding.

The car seems to be going faster. He is probably anxious to get me home before my transformation into a pumpkin is complete.

When we pull up in front of my building, I can hardly wait to get out of the car. I try to shake Jake back into consciousness and struggle with the seat belt. The awful thing seems jammed and only gives way when Mr. Barker presses the secret button.

"Listen, Celine," he says abruptly, "do you still want to visit my studio sometime?" His hand drops to my knee to keep me in the car until he has an answer. I'm sure this time. The long fingers are loosely curled. I can feel their heat through my jeans. I have to smile now to think how much he has misjudged the moment. I'm cool. Calm. I turn on him slowly so he can appreciate the scorn and contempt gathering in my voice.

"Okay," I say. "When?" I stare at him, astounded. The man must be a ventriloquist. Worse, he's making me talk like the chipmunks on Saturday-morning cartoons.

He frowns, trying to think. "I'm not sure. Why don't I give you a call? I'll call you tomorrow."

"Okay," I chirp. "That would be great!" I blink. Was that really what I wanted to say? I must be in love. That's the only explanation. In love, or possessed by cartoon characters.

Somehow I get out of the car and stagger into the building with a comatose Jacob in my arms. He is so limp and sound asleep that odd little bits threaten to fall off, but I finally deposit him in one piece with his mother.

We exchange a few words about the farm and Mr. Barker's mother's sad decline, and then she closes the door and I'm free to navigate my way into my own loft, where Catherine is filling out a questionnaire in *Cosmopolitan*.

"Hi, Catherine," I say, heading for the bathroom.

"Oh. 'lo, Celine. Celine? You got a call from . . ."

"Yeah, just a minute." I go in the bathroom, shut the door, and sit down on the edge of the tub. Okay, I ask myself. Just what, as my grandmother would say, is going on here? Is Mr. Barker really putting a move on you? In the cold clear light of Mel Hollingsford's bathroom, it doesn't seem very likely. A little hand-to-hand contact. That isn't a move, is it? And that business when I was trying to get out of the car . . . really, Gram, I'm sure that wasn't anything. I must have been unduly sensitized by a work glove . . . I have to stop and whine a bit at the memory of that glove, but then I hear my grand-mother snort.

"Why would some adult man be interested in *you?* There can be only one reason, Celine," she would say. "You just watch your step, young lady, or you'll be in deep trouble before you even know it." I lean my forehead on the cool porcelain top of the toilet tank and try to think. What is the matter with me? Why do I want to be in deep trouble before I even know it? Just consider: Mr. Barker is about five times older than I am; he is married and has a little paunch hanging over his belt. Furthermore, he is an artist, is nice to me, and has these strange hands which are very warm, with little black hairs

on the knuckles, and . . . I discover that it isn't really a
good idea to think about these things after all, so I flush
the toilet, run water in the washbowl, and go out and
ask Catherine who called.

"Some boy with a funny name. Dagwood? Dormant?
I can't remember."

"Oh. Dermot."

"Yes, that was it. Awful name, but he seemed very
nice."

"He did?"

"Yes. He tried to talk to me in French. Isn't that sweet?
He seemed very respectful. Treated me, you know, with
real respect. Not many of your friends seem anxious to
make a good impression, I've noticed. You should bring
him around some time."

"Sure. What did he want?"

"Oh, he didn't say, but he wanted you to call him
back." She glances at her watch. "I suppose it's too late
now."

"Yes," I agree. "Much too late."

FOUR /

Mr. Barker doesn't call the next day. Just as I expected. I'm sure, because I stay within twenty feet of the phone the whole time, except when I take a shower, and then I leave the door open so I can hear it ring. I'm intensely relieved, of course. And crushed. A little crushed, and by the time *Wide World of Sports* is over, a little bored. It is a good thing I have so much to occupy me during my vigil. I write Sybil and my mom letters, do some sketches of Catherine washing her hair, forget to do the revision of my paper for Mr. Carruthers. This last task consumes a lot of mental energy. Keeping the mind at the right pitch of inactivity is difficult, like learning to walk a tightrope without looking down. When I finally do remember, I am tumbling into my bed with exhaustion. Well, you idiot, I think with yet more relief. I

suppose you'll just have to go crawling to Mr. Carruthers for an extension.

The next morning in homeroom there is yet another distraction. I am informed that my advisor, Mrs. Cuddleson, wants to see me.

"What about?" I ask, but nobody knows. I must have a problem. This school is ever alert for problems. They are to be nipped in the bud, rooted out, gotten to the bottom of. They are a little like sin.

I go to Mrs. Cuddleson to have my problem identified third period. Ordinarily I would be in physical education, but this semester I am taking swimming and have been excused yet again.

The counselors' offices are in a large room on the first floor. One half of the room is divided into little cubicles whose walls don't quite reach the ceiling, so that while you are explaining why you are failing algebra you can listen to someone else speculate on what small variants in the physical laws of the universe would account for the spontaneous generation of someone else's leather jacket in the bottom of their locker. I have learned a great deal in my occasional counseling sessions.

The other half of the room is made to look like someone's living room, with a couch in the middle and a coffee table with a dish of marbles and an ivy plant. There are soft incandescent lamps which are always burning because the picture window is a fake. If a student attempted to throw him- or herself through it, they wouldn't come down in an Alpine meadow. They would hit a wall. (63)

When I walk in, the first thing I see is a short fat guy with a mobile TV unit on his shoulder, and he's talking very seriously with another guy in a tweed jacket whom I recognize right off as one of the commentators from a local network, only shorter.

The worst has happened, is my first thought. They have located Lucile Higgenbottom, and I'm going to have to find someone else to paint. There is, however, no sign of Lucile. Mrs. Cuddleson is in the living-room part of the office and she is talking to Tiffany Mortorelli and Maureen Norbert, who is combing the Farrah Fawcett wings back from her face.

I catch Mrs. Cuddleson's eye. That is, she looks at me with the expression you see on the face of people who are about to be approached by a bum who wants a quarter, and so I sit down on the bench by the door, next to a girl with blue hair. She must be a freshman, I think. She tells me she is waiting to see the nurse, but doesn't say why. Perhaps it is an infected tattoo or an impacted earring.

"What's going on?" I ask.

"They're doing a feature for Channel 9."

"A feature?"

"You know. On teen suicide."

I do know about teen suicide, as a matter of fact. Just

last night I watched a reporter interview two other reporters about the effect of reporting teen suicides on teen suicides. There have been a number of them around (64) lately, although I haven't heard of any at my school.

"Did somebody commit suicide?" I ask.

"Tiffany . . ."

We both look at Tiffany, who is tossing back her hair and lifting her chin so that the camera will pick up a good line. I am confused. Tiffany looks all right to me. The freshman gives me a jab in the ribs.

"Watch this, now. Maureen is going to talk her out of it."

"Is Tiffany really going to commit suicide?"

"Not now, you dope. It's a reexactment."

"Reenactment." I understand now. "It's called peer counseling, I think."

"Oh, yeah? Why is it called pear counseling?"

"Peer counseling. Because Tiffany and Maureen are both the same kind of people, I guess."

The freshman sniggers. "They're both fruits, you mean." Which is not exactly what I mean, but close enough.

Tiffany is just beginning to tell Maureen about how awful everything is, when Mrs. Cuddleson descends, chases the freshman out of the office, and drags me into one of the cubicles.

"Aren't you supposed to be in gym?" she asks. She sits down behind a tiny desk and shades her eyes while she leafs through a manila folder gone quite fuzzy at the edges with frequent consultations. I angle a bit, trying to make out the name typed on the file tab. Mrs. Cuddleson slaps the file closed, very deliberately.

"I said, aren't you supposed to be in physical education now?"

"Yes, but I'm excused. I'm in swimming this semester, and well, you know . . ." I hold my breath and tighten my stomach muscles in an attempt to blow the top of my head off. I hope that this will make me turn bright red. It may not be much of an expression, but it makes Miss Summers, my swimming coach, turn the color of a tomato herself and scribble on her clipboard.

Mrs. Cuddleson watches me with growing alarm. "What's wrong, Celine? Are you choking?"

"No, Mrs. Cuddleson," I say. She watches me closely as I let out my breath by slow and, I hope, imperceptible degrees. I think I confuse her sometimes.

Mrs. Cuddleson opens her file again, shielding its contents with her arm. "According to Miss Summers, you haven't attended a swimming class in the last six weeks." She cocks her eyebrows at me, the way Perry Mason does when he's closing in for the kill.

"Well, I . . ." I frown. The witness on the witness stand is having difficulty remembering.

"In fact"—isn't it the case?—"you haven't attended a single swimming class."

"Well, I guess that's right . . ." It's all coming back to me now. "But Miss Summers always excuses me."

"And always for the same reason."

Can that be? I try to look astounded, but I realize I am not being very convincing again. Actually, I'm outraged. I didn't know they were keeping statistics. Nobody had ever done this in Iowa.

There is a very sound reason why I avoid bodies of water larger than a bathtub. When I was eight months old, my mother read an article in the magazine that came with the diaper service that said babies are all natural swimmers and all sorts of problems would be avoided if they were introduced to water at an early age. My mother loves to tell the story of what happened. "She just sank!" she says, holding up her pretty hands in amazement. "She looked so sweet there, lying on the bottom of the pool, waving her little legs. Just like a little pink anemone!"

I don't remember any of this, but it must have been traumatic, mustn't it? A baby so unnatural as to sink should be kept away from water, I think. It isn't that I am a coward. If the school gave flying lessons, I would sign up in a minute. I can see us all on the roof, flapping our arms like crazy, wondering who will be the first to jump . . .

"Do you have a medical problem, Celine?" asks Mrs. Cuddleson. Her sympathy is like good picture varnish. The surface is protected, but everything shows through. "Have you seen a doctor?"

"Well, no. We don't have a doctor here. I thought when I moved to . . ."

"I think you should see a doctor, Celine. This isn't normal."

Oh. All right.

"And you might ask your doctor to send us a note."

Fair enough. I have a Mont Blanc fountain pen which I stole from my grandfather—the one in Paris—and he's a doctor. (67)

"On his letterhead."

Somewhere beyond the cubicle I hear Tiffany sobbing uncontrollably. I wonder if it is too late to try that. I suspect it is.

"You know. Address. Telephone number."

"Of course, Mrs. Cuddleson."

"It would be a pity if you had to take swimming in your senior year."

"Oh, I plan to graduate this year, Mrs. Cuddleson. You remember we talked about it. I have enough credits and everything."

"You won't graduate without your phys-ed requirement fulfilled. State law, Celine. Didn't you know? The state legislature feels that modern youth is too soft, and I think they are probably right. But everything will be okay if you complete the course." And bring a doctor's note. "And bring a doctor's note."

On the way out, I am tempted to tell Tiffany to simply get it over with. I might even offer her my X-Acto knife, which I keep in the binding of my English lit notebook. I don't. I am an understanding person who doesn't vent her own frustrations on the innocent.

After my conference with Mrs. Cuddleson I still have thirty minutes of the period to kill, so I go up to the pottery workshop and help Miss Denver load a kiln with the products of the beginning ceramics class. These are mostly Miss Piggy pencil holders.

(68)   Miss Denver is my favorite person in the school, although she occasionally breaks down and weeps. Take these pencil holders, for instance. "Use your imagination!" she cried. "Make whatever you want! Don't be afraid to be original! The world is full of ideas if you open your eyes! Look what someone made last year!"

"Oh, don't. Don't do it, Miss Denver," I murmured, panic clutching at my throat, but it was too late. She reached under her desk and brought out a Miss Piggy pencil holder. "Isn't this nice?" she said, not realizing what she had done; not hearing the vast army of Miss Piggy pencil holders marching steadily over the horizon into her life. Still, she is my favorite person, and since she is free the same hour I take swimming, I usually spend the time helping her with this and that.

I like to watch the clay or the ink or paint or whatever she's working with get spread all over her. Every now and then, she makes a conscious effort to stay clean or at least wipe the charcoal off her face before she goes out of the room, but she always forgets. I admire her for this.

She has reddish-blond hair and delicate skin, and her slanty little eyes don't have many lashes. I know that sounds terrible, but on her it looks right. Vulnerable.

She is twenty-four and this is her first job and she's having an affair with an old professor of hers down at the Art Institute, where she got her degree.

She didn't actually say that she was having an *affair*, of course, but, of course, I know. He is married, of course, and is thinking about leaving his wife, of course, so he can marry Miss Denver, of course, but it is a big step to take, of course, of course, of course. (69)

Today, as we load the Piggys into the kiln, I tell her about my problems with my swimming class and how it might actually ruin my career unless I can get this doctor's note.

"What doctor?" she says. I look at her in some surprise. I don't think she's been listening closely.

"*Any* doctor. I have to find some doctor who will say that I've got this problem that keeps me from swimming."

"Are you sick, Celine?"

This could be irritating. Where has she been for the last ten minutes?

"No, I'm not sick. That's the problem. That's why I have to find the right doctor." I'm secretly hoping, of course, that she knows just the person. But she is no help at all. When she figures out that I'm scheming to defraud the state of healthy, vigorous youth in the war against godless Communism, she turns very cool. "I don't really think you should be talking about this to me, Celine," she says. Because she is, after all, a teacher, she means. All very correct, but I'm a bit hurt. This distinction tends to be forgotten when we're alone together, cropping up again when she's feeling waxy or insecure. What is wrong now? Is the professor waffling again?

"Have you managed to fix up *Test Patterns*?" she asks,

giving my shoulder a squeeze because she knows she's being awful.

I think of *Test Patterns*, sort of loosely crucified be-
(70) tween a couple of posts in the loft so that I could study it and decide what, if anything, could be done.

"No, not exactly."

"You really should. There's going to be a show down at the Art Institute. A juried show. I'd like you to enter it. It would mean a lot if you could get accepted."

"Do you think I could? Really?"

Miss Denver shrugs. "Well. It depends on the jury, of course. These things are always a gamble, and it doesn't mean a thing if you're rejected, but I do think you might have a chance."

Wow. And I've destroyed the thing. It might still be made into a good painting, but it's never going to be *Test Patterns* again. That's gone. I consider for a second trying to make a copy of the original, but that is weakness, not to mention impossible.

"When do you have to submit stuff? I mean, I'm working on some new things. I'm going to make a portrait of Lucile Higgenbottom, and there's some other stuff. Maybe I could submit those."

"Maybe. But why not *Test Patterns?*"

Fortunately, I don't have to answer this, because at that moment the telephone in Miss Denver's little office in the corner of the studio rings. She is off and running in a second.

I maneuver close enough to hear her side of the conversation, even though she keeps her back turned away.

"No," she says. "Yes . . . No . . . I can't talk now. Yes. I understand."

Not very revealing, but I think I'm right. The professor (71) is getting cold feet.

When Miss Denver comes back, she works with a great show of efficiency for about two minutes.

"Hey!" I say. "Be careful." She has just put in two pigs touching. If they had been fired that way, they would have stuck together. "You'll make Siamese-twin Miss Piggy pencil holders."

I check her face for a smile, and her naked eyes are filled with tears. While I watch, they start spilling over and running down her cheeks. They make little runnels in the charcoal there. It is the saddest thing I have ever seen in my life.

"That bad?" I ask. She nods, and starts dabbing at the corners of her eyes with the back of her wrist.

"He's decided not to leave his wife?" I should keep my mouth shut, but I am really interested. She fumbles in her pocket for a tissue that she's obviously been using all morning.

"No, no. They're getting a . . . It's just so . . . so messy. And there's the child."

The child? I didn't know there was a child.

"I wonder," I say. "I wonder if he's like this guy my mother was going with one time. Brad Donnelly? You might have heard of him because he used to be this big record producer. Anyway, he and my mom decide that he'll leave his wife, who *was* sort of awful really, and get married, but then months go by and nothing happens, and my mom is really getting desperate because she has this idea that if she can only marry Brad then her life will be perfect. And finally I say, 'Well, if you do marry him, he's not giving *me* any baths.' And she says, 'What do you mean, baths?' And I say, 'Well, all I know is that every time I go over there he always ends up giving Cam a bath.' It was true, too. He had this damp kid named Cam that I used to play with. The poor kid was practically waterlogged. He was always after me to take a bath, too, and it was tempting, because they had this great Jacuzzi, but I decided it wasn't worth it.

"Anyway, my mom turns practically white, and she asks in this real scared voice, 'Does he touch her?' And I say, 'Of course he touches her. He *washes* her.' And then my mother doesn't say anything for a while, but just walks around the apartment for about ten hours, giving me these really funny looks every now and then . . ."

While I am jabbering on and giving her the benefit of my experience, I am also smoothing out a rough spot on a Miss Piggy snout, and so I don't notice that she has this most peculiar expression on her face—Miss Denver, not Miss Piggy—until it is too late.

"Celine, I . . . you . . ." She waggles her hands helplessly. "Celine, I think it's been very wrong of me to have talked about these things with you. I'm really very, very sorry, but I think maybe you should go back to your other class now. I'm sorry. I'll try to explain, but I can't right now. Do you understand?"

"Yes," I say, and I turn around and walk out. In the hall I start to blubber. It isn't what she said. It's the way she looked at me. It was a very strange expression, a mix of pity and horror. As if I was a monster of some kind. (73) What had I said or done to make her look at me that way? It's a kind of shock, and while I bumble on down the hall, I keep thinking, That's what you are, you know. A kind of monster. Why is that so? Why am I a monster?

After school Dermot consoles me at Wendy's with a cheeseburger and large fries. He notices that I've been crying, and although I can't tell him why, he is happy enough speculating. He assumes naturally that it has something to do with him, that my stepmother is putting obstacles in his path. He can't understand it. When he talked to her on the phone, he really turned on the old charm. "I really turned on the old charm" is the way he puts it. He has lots of questions about Mr. Barker, too, having heard that I had spent Saturday frolicking in the countryside with him. He still shows signs of jealousy even after I explain about the wheelchair and the portable oxygen tank, but he's reasonably chipper. Perhaps because I allow him to feed me. Dermot apparently believes that food is the royal road to seduction. Perhaps he is right. I am both ravenous and pathetically grateful. Even a monster must be fed.

Lucile is happy, too. She arrives at our table, dragging Philip by the hand. A butterfly airlifting a frog.

"Hey, I can go to the party with you," she says. "As long as we stay together at all times. You have to come to supper Thursday so my mom can meet you. Wear a dress and try not to act like a complete jerk." These may not be her exact words. It is the gist of her message, however.

(74)   "What about the portrait?"

"Portrait?"

"Of you. You said you would pose for me."

"Oh, yeah. Well. Maybe next weekend. Is that okay?"

I must be satisfied with this vague promise and the delight of Dermot, who is cavorting around the restaurant with the grace of a Saint Bernard.

FIVE /

After I leave Dermot at Wendy's, I am walking toward the bus stop, thinking about all I've eaten and the way Miss Denver looked when I told her about Brad Donnelly bathing his little daughter, when suddenly I get slapped in the head with this absolutely terrific idea. I'm watching a bus kneel down to pick up an old lady with her aluminum walker, and I'm absolutely staggered. I careen through the line of people waiting to get on the bus and keep walking. I have to think about this, and I can't do that, fumbling for my bus pass.

A self-portrait. Celine-Monster. No. Beast. Celine-Beast. A body like a tree trunk with the bark peeled off, little flappy titties like pasties, and great stone feet. Wings. Comic-page orange, and like an outfielder's mitt with fleshy feathers. They wouldn't lift a bat off the ground. (76) Thalidomide wings sprouting right out of the shoulder sockets instead of arms, and totally useless. A flat, confused face, and a big blurry mouth with pretty, pretty red lips, but a hungry mouth snapping at double cheeseburgers, flour burritos, stuffed pizzas. French fries and chocolate-covered cherries coming down like hail out of a pink sky, and all the food slick and glistening with fat. Airbrushed highlights, or maybe the reflections plugged in like tiny distorted windows of pure shine.

I catch up with the bus at the next stop and hop on, thinking it will get me home faster, but it is hardly moving at all through the traffic and I keep bouncing up and down to make it go faster until I realize that the little old lady with the aluminum walker sitting across the aisle is afraid I'm going to wet my pants, and so I become calm.

I'm not going to lose this, I tell myself. This is a very tough idea. A very strong one. It's not going to fade on me, get all soggy like cornflakes left too long in the bowl. It will triumph over boredom, depression, falling in love, cold sores, headaches, homework, other people, all the things that conspire against getting a painting together. The only thing I have to worry about is dying before it is finished. A familiar flutter of panic begins somewhere down in my stomach. What if the bus should run into a gasoline truck before I get home? What if international terrorists have already introduced bubonic plague into

America's soft-drink supply? It doesn't matter, I tell my-self. This is the way you want to go when the time comes, bursting with an idea that's going to grow up and be a disappointment, anyway.

By the time I arrive at my front door I am in control, almost serene. My life is arranged. My early, tragic death anticipated and accepted. I compose moving obituaries as I climb the stairs, one precise step at a time. Promising Artist Struck Down as Career Is About to . . . to . . . to Blossom? Boil Over? Burst? "It is practically impossible to gauge the loss to American art," comments Angelica Denver, local artist and teacher. "A child perhaps, but a soul of such depth . . . and . . . and . . ."

When I open the door I find that Catherine is already home. This is a surprise. Lately she has been spending her afternoons at the library or the Art Institute, slogging away on her thesis on the late drawings of Vincent van Gogh, or so she says. Today, however, she is painting her toenails, balanced precariously on a kitchen chair, her feet on the table, little wads of cotton wool between her toes. A delicate smell of shrimp curry fills the air.

" 'lo, Catherine. What's going on? What are you doing here?"

"I'm painting my toenails."

"Yeah. Can I do it?"

Catherine grunts and surrenders the bottle. "What is it with you and painting toenails?" she asks, to make it clear that she's the one doing the favor.

"I don't know. I like feet, I guess. Maybe it's the challenge of staying in the lines." The truth is, I see a paint-brush in somebody's hand and I immediately want to take over. There are only three toes left, which is a disappointment.

When I'm finished, I step back and admire the result. It's easy to see that those three toes were done by a master. "You want me to do the others over?" I ask hopefully.

"Don't be ridiculous. I've got a million things to do. We're having company for dinner. Do you think you could take a bath or something? You're a bit earthy today."

"Sure. Who's coming?" This is very interesting. Apparently Catherine has been out there meeting people, having coffee, doing things. My assumption that she ceases to exist when not standing immediately before my eyes is apparently mistaken.

"Professor Merkie . . ."

"Who's Professor Merkie?"

"You know. He teaches art history at Circle."

"Oh," I say, still doubtful about ever having heard of Professor Merkie, but I suddenly remember Celine-Beast and feel a twinge of guilt because I've been distracted by as small a thing as three toes in need of paint. "Great. Wonderful. I can hardly wait to meet him," I assure her, and get out my 48-by-24-inch newsprint pad and flop down on the floor. Great, lumpy weight-lifter shoulders is what I want. Leathery skin half an inch thick like the skin on Michelangelo sculptures. I love that thick, thick skin.

Catherine hobbles around on her heels, arranging dried weeds and flowers at strategic places, but I won't be distracted now. I dig my piece of compressed charcoal into the paper. Every line has a shape.

"Celine. I just vacuumed in here. Is that really necessary?"

"Yes. Absolutely necessary." I pull off my T-shirt and feel my shoulder muscles. Shoulders are practically impossible.

"Catherine? Would you do me a favor and take off your dress? I want to see your shoulder muscles."

"Celine! Get your shirt on! There are people coming."

"Just five minutes. I want to feel your bones," I say, leaping up and following her around, trying to get hold of her shoulders.

"Stop it, Celine! Your hands are filthy! You are an absolute lunatic." She casts about for some way to fend off the inspired artist. "You got a letter!" she screeches desperately.

"Later," I say, advancing upon her grimly, already anticipating the sound of those pathetic whimpers.

"From Sybil!"

"From Sybil?" That's different. "Where is it? Where has she been? What's she been doing?"

"She's been in Costa Rica. Digging latrines." Of course. Costa Rica. Digging latrines. Sybil is . . . I must think for a moment. Even the most elementary description of Sybil requires thought, she is so difficult to place in this world. She is the daughter, first of all, of the only man I ever wished my mother would marry, and Sybil and I might never have met if my mother had not sprained an ankle climbing the prehistoric battlements of Maiden Castle near Salisbury Plain and been rescued by the last man in the world to wear detachable collars. He always seemed a very ordinary man to me. Perhaps he felt that way about himself and that is why he went to such trouble to have shirts made without collars so that he could attach his own. It is difficult to believe that anyone who in some small bid for immortality stands in front of a mirror each morning and struggles with shirt studs could be Sybil's father, and yet it is so.

After he had rescued my mother and assisted her to his car, he invited her to his house in the country, and since they could hardly drive off and leave me there all alone with the skeletons of the brave Britons who had died defending their homeland from the Roman invaders, I was invited, too. The house was big and grand, and I discovered in ten minutes a young woman trying to incorporate improvements of her own design in the sanitary arrangements for the pheasants kept in a run at the bottom of the garden.

"Take hold of that pipe!" were her first words to me. "Hold it! Hold it! You little weed!" she added, and then, when the pipe was properly fixed, she put a dung-coated hand squarely on top of my head and said, "You'll do." Her name was Sybil, and I fell in love at once.

No one is surprised that I love Sybil, of course. Nearly everyone does, except my father. The marvel is that apparently Sybil loves me, too. No one knows why. It is an absolute marvel, people keep saying, marveling. But it is one of the few things I am really sure of. Even when I try to sit on her lap and drool all over her, her love (81) remains unshaken. If I was drowning in the middle of the ocean, I would be able to relax. I would struggle until I was exhausted and then relax, knowing that in a moment I would feel Sybil's hand on my collar pulling me up. She would wipe the water out of my eyes and kiss me on the forehead. I would believe this past all waiting.

I don't see her very often. Sometimes I don't even know where she is. But she writes to me on blue airmail stationery that is often torn and punctured by the stiff probing nib of her pen. Her letters are always about me. She has dreamed about me, or eaten a *madeleine* and been reminded of the afternoon we scratched our bare legs in the blackberries, or she has come across my hands in a brothel for little girls in Manila. Her letters are full of admonitions, analysis, contradictions. I feel I am never out of her thoughts. Lately she has been working for a world health organization. She must be very tired. It is such exhausting work to save the world. If only she would be content merely to save me.

Catherine finally finds Sybil's letter in a pile of junk mail. It has a bright red seal on the flap, which I admire until I realize it is toenail paint. Catherine has apparently been using it as a blotter.

"Hey! It's been opened!" I protest.

"If you look at the front, you'll see that it's addressed

to both of us," Catherine says. "She wants to enlist my support in this crazy idea of your going to visit her this summer."

(82) "Crazy? What's crazy about that? I thought it was all settled."

"Settled? For God's sakes, Celine. We've been over this a million times. You know your father said it was out of the question." I do as a matter of fact have a faint recollection of some such thoughtless phrase being bantered about, but this was just his first reaction. His establishing of a skirmishing line, so to speak. One of the great drawbacks of his having rushed off on this lecture tour is that I haven't yet had the chance really to mop up the initial resistance.

"Well, what am I supposed to do? Hang around here all summer? With you?" I say, bringing out some pretty powerful weapons right away. Strike hard, strike fast. I loom over her in a fair imitation of General Patton. I can tell she is shaken, her mental processes in disarray.

"I think he plans to send you to that camp. Where you can learn German."

"German! I can't learn German. It would corrupt me. I would develop terminal glottal stop!"

"What? Celine, it is impossible for me to make any sense of you at all. We're not going to discuss it further. You can talk to your father if you want," she says, and runs off to the bathroom to put on her makeup for Professor Merkie. See? She's in retreat already. I really am going to visit Sybil. All I have to do is show a little maturity. And persistence. Yes. Maturity and persistence are my watchwords. I carry off Sybil's letter to my futon to enjoy.

It is a wonderful letter, as usual, full of helpful advice (83) about bringing my father around. There is a picture of me enclosed. It is a postcard from the Uffizi Gallery, and I am dressed in the costume of a Florentine nobleman's daughter of the fifteenth century. Sybil draws particular attention to the set of my mouth. Determined, settled. A young woman capable of subverting the laws of nature to get what she wants. I am busy practicing the expression and feeling power seep into my bones when the doorbell rings. It is Jake and his mother. Mrs. Barker and Catherine confer at the door and Jacob, after determining that the television is off, comes over to see what I'm doing.

"Can I come up," he says, fingering my personal ladder. I give my permission, regally, and he climbs up. I favor him with my new expression. Disdain and contempt.

"What's the matter with you?" he asks, giving me a punch. Rats. I'll have to practice in front of a mirror or check up on what actually happened to that Florentine nobleman's daughter. Probably her parents or family friends poisoned her.

"Nothing." I take a careful peep out of my bed at Mrs. Barker, who is shaking her head while Catherine mutters at her. "What's your mom want?"

"I don't know. Hey, this swings," says Jake, admiring my futon.

"Yeah. To do it right, you have to put your feet on the ceiling. Take off your shoes. We're in my bed, you know." By lying on top of me, he's able to get his short little legs up high enough. We swing gently. Now there are two sets of footprints on the ceiling. I hope he appreciates this honor.

"Celine?" Catherine calls. Mrs. Barker has disappeared. "Could you and Jacob come down here? I want you to do something for me. Go to the bakery and buy some stuff. Some raspberry tarts. The little ones. Four should be enough."

"Okay. Later," I say, climbing down. "I've got this picture I'm working on."

"And you can take Jacob with you. Now."

I am about to object to this plan when I see that Catherine is making meaningful faces at me. She explains when she sends Jacob to the toilet.

"Jacob's bloody awful father is coming over this afternoon sometime," she whispers.

So? It's about time. I've been very patient.

"He's coming to get his *things*."

This sounds serious. When people start coming around to get their *things*, I know they are simply detouring on their way to the lawyer. "Jacob's mother asked if we could keep him out of the way for a while. It would be better if he wasn't here."

I'm not persuaded of this, but there is no time to argue, because Jacob has returned and wants to know if this bakery we are going to gives cookies to little children. I promise that we will find out, and Catherine slips me some cash and suggests that since Professor Merkie won't arrive before six, it'll be fine if Jacob and I stop by the playground and play on the swings. Excellent. We will swing on the swings.

I shouldn't be sarcastic, because actually we have an interesting time. The bakery doesn't give cookies to little children, but they'll sell them to anyone, and we buy enough to keep us occupied while we sit on a bench in the park and draw patterns in the dirt with the toes of our sneakers and talk about Life. Jacob seems to know as much as anyone, although he is annoyed because no one will tell him why his parents have separated. He keeps asking, but they won't say.

"Maybe they don't know why," I suggest, but he's not satisfied with this, being too young to understand that it might be true.

"Dr. Korbel won't tell me, either," he says. "She always wants to talk about other stuff." Dr. Korbel is the counselor that he's been going to see on Saturday mornings to help him deal with the problems created by his parents' separation.

"Oh," I say. "Well, what stuff does Dr. Korbel talk about?"

"Well, you know . . ." he begins, and I do know, too. I've never actually been to a psychologist myself, but I've heard it all somewhere or another. All about how much his parents both love him, and how they weren't separating from him but just from each other. They would always love him and the important thing is that it isn't his fault. Sometimes little boys and girls think that they've made their mommy and daddy mad and that's why they're

separating, but that isn't it at all. They love their kid and always will, forever and ever.

He tells me all this in a little singsong voice, nodding his head from side to side in time to the music, and then he looks at me with eyes that don't expect anything anymore and waits for me to say, "Well, she's right. Dr. Korbel's right."

I can't say it. I want to but I can't, because it will be like throwing up. This stuff will come out of my mouth and stick to my lips like Silly Putty, and then I'll have to go around forever with this lie hanging out of my face.

"What a bunch of crap," I say.

Do I really mean that, even after I've had a second to think about it? I think I do. I mean, this counselor's talking as if his parents' separation has nothing to do with Jake. As if it was a nearby natural disaster, a close brush with death. As if a jet plane was heading his way five feet off the ground. "It's scary," she's saying, "but you don't have to worry, because you're so short. It's going to miss you by two feet, and you won't even feel the breeze." But that isn't the way it is at all. His parents don't like their lives anymore, and they're willing to chop the kid up a bit to change things. That's the truth, isn't it? If they really loved him so much, they wouldn't get a divorce. No, you might as well face it, Jacob. Family life is over. You're just not worth it.

I don't say any of this, of course. I would probably be struck dead by the god of self-fulfillment if I did, but I must have said enough, because when I look at Jacob he's staring at me, mouthing the word.

"What's the matter," I say. He looks so wild I'm a little scared.

"Crap," he says. He gets up and marches back and forth in front of me. "Crap! Crap! Crap!" he shouts louder and louder, squeezing his eyes shut and pounding with his hands in the air.

"Hey, Jake," I say, and try to catch him as he goes by. He turns and with his eyes still closed starts pounding me, hitting me in the breast so hard that I have to grab him before I faint. "Crap! Crap! Crap!"

I hold him tight so he won't hurt me anymore. "I'm sorry, Jake. I'm so, so sorry."

We get calmed down after a few minutes. I mean both of us, because for some reason I'm very upset, too. We choke down a few more cookies to soak up the tears, and then we really do go and swing on the swings.

"Higher!" Jake keeps yelling, even after he goes into free fall at the top of each swing until the chains catch him with a jerk. The supports of the swing with their great wads of subterranean cement are pulling right out of the ground, but we're not afraid. We're flying, in a way.

SIX /

It is after six when Jake and I get back to our apartment building, but we are still too early or just in time, depending on how you look at it. A U-Haul van is pulled up in front, and Mr. Barker is coming down the steps with an armload of cardboard boxes.

I wonder what we are going to say to each other. I mean, I've been rehearsing. (Mr. Barker: "Oh, Celine, I've been trying to call you, but there must be something wrong with my phone. Some conspiracy by AT&T . . ." Me: "You've been trying to call? I was afraid of that. I've been so busy doing all my various things that I've hardly been home at all . . .") But the script suddenly looks a little tatty. I shouldn't have worried, because he doesn't say anything to me at all.

"What are you *doing?*" Jake yells, charging down the sidewalk.

"Hi, Jacob." Mr. Barker heaves his boxes over the bumper of the van and then squats down and tries to hug Jake. "How's my trooper?"

"Okay, but what are you *doing?*" Jake almost stiff-arms his father in his worry about what's going in the back of the truck.

"Just moving some stuff. Some stuff I need." Mr. Barker stands up slowly and rubs his elbows.

"Why do you need that? You don't need that," Jake wails. Mr. Barker simply shakes his head. Maybe he can hardly believe himself that he should need so much.

"I've got a few more things upstairs," he says to me. "You want to help?"

Mrs. Barker watches from the landing as we climb the stairs together. She looks very pretty in old blue jeans and with her hair held back by a red bandanna. So pretty that I have for a moment a loony vision that she will suddenly smile and come down the steps to meet us, holding out her pale arms to gather us in. As we get close she retreats slowly, and then turns abruptly and walks into *my* apartment. This confuses me, and while I'm trying to decide what to do I follow Jacob and his father into the loft across the hall. We trudge in a sort of lockstep. I feel like we are shackled together.

Everything in Jacob's place is white. The walls and

floors, the canvas sofas and the low plastic tables. Every book in the white Erector-set bookcases has a homemade white dust jacket. White curtains bleach the late-after-noon sun. It's the scariest place I've ever seen in my life.

Jacob and his father don't even seem to notice that I'm there. Mr. Barker is busy trying to dismantle an enormous studio easel, and Jacob is bouncing around the room like a yo-yo on a rubber string.

"What are you doing?" he keeps asking, opening card-board boxes, putting his hands on the easel, not to help, but as if he could somehow keep his father from carrying it away. "Why are you taking it? You need it here."

"Now, Jacob," says his father. "Act your age." He nails his son to one spot with a very severe frown, and Jacob stays there and wrings his hands until his father tries to pull a big plastic bag over one of those adjustable chairs that ride you up and down.

"Don't take that," says Jacob very gently and tries to restrain his father's hands.

"Jacob! It's my drafting chair. I need it."

"No! You gave it me! You gave it me!" Jacob says and begins to cry.

His father stands there looking very helpless for a min-ute and then he turns and says to me, "Would you mind taking Jacob in to his mother now, please?"

It is not necessary. At the mention of his mother Jake runs out of the loft and Mr. Barker and I are left alone. The silence is so thick it is like white noise.

He opens a small cabinet and begins to sort its contents

between a cardboard box and a plastic garbage bag. There are dried and twisted tubes of paint, cans of varnish and oil, frayed brushes and scabby palette knives. In the white room they all look filthy and soiled beyond use. Still, at first he seems sure of himself. To know his own mind. This he wants to save, this to throw out. He frowns. A little sheen of sweat appears on his forehead. He begins to hesitate, to be unable to decide. His hands waver, his possessions twist in his grip, until finally a jar of poster paint slips from his fingers and smashes on the floor between the box and the plastic bag. I'm almost bounced into the air by the sharp crack of it, and on the way down I grab for a roll of paper towels, because disorder is not to be borne, not in this place.

"Leave it!" he says sharply.

We stare at the splash of paint. It is small, but red, as if the floor had begun to bleed. "Just leave it. I can't stand fuss."

He dumps the rest of the stuff from the cabinet into the plastic bag and looks at me. "I'm sorry. I seem to be always shouting at the wrong person. Let me have the paper towels. I'd better get this cleaned up." He sniffs morosely at the paint. "I'm leaving enough messes behind as it is."

We get down on our knees, wiping at the spill together.

"I was supposed to call you, wasn't I?" he says after a moment.

"No. That's okay."

"No, I'm sorry. I didn't forget, it's just that my life

seems a little complicated right now. I mean, I'm trying
to move and my studio's full of junk . . . And then there's
this other person . . . We seem to be having trouble
communicating right now."

"No, really," I say quickly. I don't want to hear about
this other person. "This week is terrible for me, too. I've
got all this schoolwork piling up like sandbags. I mean,
there's this paper that I've absolutely got to get done last
Monday, and I'm going to this dance Thursday . . ."

"No kidding? A dance? A prom, is it?"

"No, just a dance. The International Relations Club.
What's the matter? Is that funny?" I ask, all prickly and
ready to take offense because he has this big smile on his
face.

"No! That's not funny." He turns wistful. "That's not
funny at all."

"Well, it's not exactly the high point of my life, but
it would be okay if I didn't have to go with Dermot." I
am ready to explain to Mr. Barker just what is wrong
with Dermot if he's interested, but he is not. He starts
wadding up all the paper towels and shoving them into
his garbage bag.

"Well," he says. "I'm sorry we can't get together. It
would have been fun."

"Yeah. It's too bad."

"But really impossible this week."

"Oh, absolutely. I mean, I've got so much to do I need
a time machine."

"To make more time, you mean? Yeah."

"Yeah," I say, pleased to learn that I haven't been reduced to complete nonsense. We stare at the floor together. It is completely clean. Not a spot of paint anywhere. Not a speck. No, not even a faint blush. I'm not sure how long I can stand here not breathing and admiring the floor. Forever, it must be.

"How about Saturday?" he says.

"Saturday?"

"Yeah. I'm painting my studio. I think I'm going to move in there. You want to help me paint the walls?"

"Paint the walls?"

"Green. Institutional green. Or maybe puce." He sighs and looks around the room. "Anything but white."

"Okay. When?"

"I don't know. Lunchtime? We could have lunch."

"Lunch?"

"Yes. You have time to eat lunch, don't you? Here." He writes down the address of his studio on a scrap of paper towel and puts it in my hand. We get carefully to our feet without looking at each other once. I feel as if we've just agreed to rob a bank.

"See!" I hear Jake cry. "He's taking all our stuff!" He's standing in the doorway, tugging at the waistband of his mother's jeans. She sways slightly as she watches us.

"It's his stuff," she says in a flat voice. "He needs it."

"But why is he taking it? He needs it here!"

"No, he doesn't. He's not going to live here anymore. We talked about that. Don't you remember?"

"But why? Why isn't he going to live here anymore?"

She doesn't answer. Perhaps Jake is the only person in the world still interested in this question. She rouses herself with an effort and peers into a box of flattened rolls of paper and empty mailing tubes.

"What's this?" she asks.

Mr. Barker glances at the box. His fingers are entangled in the strips of masking tape with which he is trying to fasten down the plastic bag over his drafting chair. "Some old stuff. I'll sort it out later."

Mrs. Barker extracts one of the rolls and tries to open it out. It resists her efforts. The paper no longer has any memory of being something flat and pliable. It wants to stay curled, like a dried secret.

"Hold it here," she orders me, and between us we stretch out a watercolor. A seascape, full of watery light and shadows. In the distance is a lighthouse. A bit of flinty white.

"It's one of those sketches you did on Casco Bay," Mrs. Barker announces. "It's ruined now. All creased."

"It doesn't matter. It wasn't any good."

"You used to think it was marvelous. You were going to be another Winslow Homer, don't you remember?"

"I never said it was marvelous."

"Oh no, of course not. You were too modest. But I knew. You used to be so proud, bringing your little sketches home in the evening. We'd spread them out on the porch and drink gin and tonics and I'd have to persuade you that they were beautiful. You already thought so, but I had to persuade you anyway. I was very good at that, wasn't I? I always knew exactly what to say."

"I was going in the wrong direction," says Mr. Barker quietly. "It was all wrong. I was too busy trying to please others, and forgot what I wanted to do myself." He doesn't look at his wife. It's just as well. Her eyes are filled with an awful rage.

"Can I have it?" Jake asks, peering at the painting over his mother's elbow.

"What? Oh no, darling. Your father has to throw it away. It isn't worth saving. You heard what he said. He was going in the wrong direction. I'm not sure exactly what that means. It makes art sound like a traffic pattern, doesn't it? But all this is worthless. It has to be swept away." She snatches the painting from my fingers and tries to sail it across the room like a Frisbee, but it snaps back into a roll in midair and lands with a brittle klunk at Mr. Barker's feet. He picks it up and glances at me. "I don't think this little show is necessary, Jean."

Mrs. Barker blinks at him innocently. "Because of Celine, you mean? But she's a painter, too. She should know." She catches my hands. "Listen, Celine," she whispers breathlessly. "There comes a time in a painter's life when he feels stifled. He can't say why exactly, but he feels he can no longer grow. Isn't that amazing? He may have a decent job and a family, but that isn't enough. They crush all of his creativity.

"Now the important thing to remember is that if this happens to you, then you have to break free. You have to start over. Find people who aren't dull and demanding and who understand just how important it is that your artistic gifts be appreciated. People with whom you've lived a long time . . . they forget that. They forget just how wonderful you really are. They start wanting things themselves. And they're always the same. Boring and (96) dull. Complaining about the vacuuming or wanting you to help with the dishes. This holds you back. You just have to get rid of these people and start all over."

She pauses and looks at me. Her smile turns hesitant, as if she was telling me a joke and was no longer sure I would understand.

"Oh, dear," she says, throwing up her white hands. "I'm not being very convincing, am I? It all sounds so selfish when I try to explain. You should ask Paul about it. It's all very clear when he says it. It sounds so reasonable. So noble. Isn't that true, Paul?"

Mr. Barker ignores her. "Come here, Jacob," he says, squatting down and spreading out the watercolor so that he and Jake can look at it together. "You really like this? You can have it. You can have all this stuff. You see this lighthouse? It's called Halfway Rock Light. I never was out there myself, but your mother used to go with Desmond Brasneiger. He had this sailboat. A Bluejay it was, and there was just room for two."

Mrs. Barker turns as white as her floors, her walls, her book jackets. She looks at me. "Catherine asked me to send you home, Celine. Your company has arrived."

I unhook my eyes from hers—a delicate operation—and work my way through a maze of furniture to the door.

*   *   *

"Paul Barker . . ." mutters Theodore Merkie as he explores his curry with his fork. "The name is familiar, but . . . What's he do?"

"I'm not really sure," says Catherine. She watches anxiously as the professor discovers a small pink lump and maneuvers it to the edge of his plate. "Abstractions, I think. Large. On unstretched canvas."

"That's not a scallop, is it?" asks Mrs. Merkie, peering into her husband's supper. "We have to be so careful. Ted and scallops don't agree, if you know what I mean. When we were on the Costa Brava last March, Ted ate a scallop. We had checked with the waiter, of course, but the man mustn't have understood. Anyway . . ." As she talks, her husband's head begins to bob and weave with annoyance.

"Mother!" he says sharply. "No one's interested!"

"It's a shrimp. No scallops," says Catherine quickly, but the professor continues to glare at his wife, until she wilts back in her chair and dabs at her lips with a napkin. The professor turns back to his plate, scraping at the lump with his fork.

"Come to think of it," he says, "I did see a few of Barker's things at Art Expo last . . . last . . . Not very memorable. He showed some promise a few years back. I was able to advise one of my more affluent friends—someone who doesn't have to make do on a poor scholar's salary—on acquiring one or two . . . one or two things. Quite nice. Doubled in value, I should think. But then the gallery crowd got to him. Barker, I mean. Hasn't done anything interesting since. Too anxious to please the powers that be. Ended up looking like a second-rate . . . a second-rate . . ."

"Rothko," suggests Catherine. "I do remember being disappointed. His work seemed so derivative. There didn't seem to be any ideas which Rothko hasn't explored much more deeply."

The professor is staring at her in astonishment. "Rothko!" he barks.

"Well," says Catherine, turning pink. "His palette, I mean. Those violets and oranges. That *soiled* look." The professor's indignation endures, threatens to solidify, but then he relents and turns back to his curry. The lump is indeed a shrimp. He pokes at it tentatively, and then abruptly snaps it up into his mouth.

"Possibly," he concedes. "One thinks of Diebenkorn first, of course. It's evident in the color edges."

"Oh, of course. You see that at once," Catherine says. All the ladies relax. Conversation with Professor Merkie is fraught with hazards. His opinions litter the conversation like land mines, ready to explode at a touch, little eruptions of contempt. I was stunned into silence hours ago, and Mrs. Merkie talks largely to herself. Mutters of admonition, an occasional wry twist of the lips at something Catherine says.

Over the salad, Professor Merkie gives us a lecture about the state of contemporary art. His vision is tragic. He sees no way out. It's the culture, he explains. Emasculated by cultural relativism, feminism, television, and, in some way that I don't quite grasp, teachers' unions.

"No," he concludes. "We're at a low ebb in the cultural tide. So much art. All of it bad. The wellsprings of genuine creativity are dry. All that a modern artist can do is parody the aspirations of the past." He beams with satisfaction. He likes that last line and repeats it twice. I feel my face assuming its fascinated-idiot expression. Eyes slightly crossed, coated tongue protruding between slack lips.

I am startled when Mrs. Merkie says brightly, "Present company excluded, of course." For a moment no one knows what she is talking about. "Ted and I were admiring your work, Celine, before you arrived," she explains. "We think your paintings are marvelous. Isn't that so, Ted?"

Professor Merkie gives the walls the once-over, like a contractor estimating how much it would cost to paper them. There are a few things there that I have forgotten to take down. I will them to spontaneously combust, but they simply curl at the corners.

"Oh, yes," says the professor. "Very nice."

What a relief. The words every artist wants to hear. It's hard to know how to respond. I consider tipping over backwards in my chair and lying there with my feet in the air, overwhelmed by the glory of it all, but Catherine nails me down with eyes as sharp as needles.

"Rothko . . ." the professor says quietly, reverting to an earlier subject of conversation. "Really an overrated painter, don't you think? I liked that observation of yours, Catherine. About the soiled look of his canvas. Catches that quality." He moistens his lips to elaborate, but doesn't go far. "Like soiled linen," he says, a faraway look in his eyes.

Catherine beams and Mrs. Merkie bristles.

"That doesn't seem right to me at all," she says. Her hands tremble as she arranges the crumbs by her plate with dry, freckled fingers. "I've always loved his paintings. They have some magic . . . something that speaks directly to . . . to people's feelings. You don't have to be an expert to feel it. It has nothing to do with underwear or . . . underwear." She falters as she watches the professor and Catherine exchange knowing smiles. The professor seems to expand slightly, swelling up like a toad in his neat blue suit. It is really too much to bear.

"I think you're absolutely right," I say. "Rothko's great. It doesn't have anything to do with what you said." In fact, I don't even understand how underwear worked its way into the conversation, but I am as one with Mrs. Merkie in keeping it in its place.

Catherine stiffens with alarm, but the professor smiles indulgently. "That's the popular opinion of Rothko, Celine," he says. "But as you get a little older and learn something more about art, I'll wager your opinion will change."

"No, it won't," I say. "Or, if it does, then that will be too bad, because then I'll be wrong."

"It seems you don't have much trust in education."

"It's a tricky thing. A lot of people spend a lot of time getting dumber and dumber."

"Present company excepted, of course," flutters Mrs. Merkie uncertainly. I know I should shut up, and I would, too, if the professor didn't have to have the last word.

"Oh dear," he says with a fluty laugh. "I think we have here an advocate of the innocent eye."

"No, we don't," I say, not the least bit interested in what an advocate of the innocent eye is. Probably something dirty, I tell myself. Like soiled linen. The truth is that I'm not very good at arguments. I tend to get excited and then rattled and proceed rapidly from direct contradiction to personal insult.

Catherine knows this, and begins to clatter dishes together with abandon. "Is everyone finished? Why don't we have some dessert now?" she cries gaily. She challenges me with her eyes to say just one more word, and although I am not easily intimidated, the thought of the raspberry tarts subdues me.

"The curry was absolutely delicious," says Mrs. Merkie, helping Catherine with the salad plates. "All those clever spices and things. I don't know how you do it."

"It's quite simple, really. You just have to know how to read a cookbook," says Catherine. She looks annoyed by the compliment for some reason.

"Oh, don't say that. Not many young women are so handy around the kitchen these days. You mustn't hide your talents under a bushel." Mrs. Merkie lapses into deep thought, a lemony smile fixed on her face, until Catherine returns with a few hard pears and a sagging lump of Camembert cheese.

"Where're the tarts?" I ask in alarm.

"Tarts?"

"Yeah. You know. The ones I bought at the bakery."

"Oh. Those. Do you really want a sweet?" she asks brightly of Professor and Mrs. Merkie. "They looked a bit sick-making to me."

"Not for me, thank you," says the professor, whittling away at a pear. "Never understood this American passion for gooey sweets. Why spoil things? This is perfect. A perfect conclusion to a perfect meal."

"No, it isn't," I say, ready to do battle again. But the professor merely frowns.

"Come help me with the coffee, Celine," says Catherine, applying an affectionate chokehold and guiding me into the kitchen.

There, in furious whispers, we conduct an autopsy on my behavior.

"What in heaven's name is the matter with you? Why can't you behave? We're having a perfectly ordinary conversation, and you have to start acting like a yahoo. It's absolutely humiliating."

"No, it isn't. And it wasn't an ordinary conversation. He's awful. He says all these dumb things about art, and he's mean to his wife."

"His wife?" Catherine reels with astonishment. "She's not his wife! She's his mother! Where did you get the idea that she's his wife?" The enormity of my mistake seems to cheer her up. She almost giggles as she measures coffee into the large espresso pot. She can't get over it. "Didn't you hear him call her Mother? Really, Celine. I think you're losing contact with reality."

"So what if he calls her Mother? Uncle John calls Aunt Etty Mother all the time." This is a fact. It drives Aunt Etty wild.

"Professor Merkie is not an Iowa farmer. I think when he calls someone Mother you can be fairly sure that that's who it is."

"I know he's not an Iowa farmer. I know that. You know what? When I first saw him I thought he was a store detective. Somebody you met at Marshall Field's. He has that look, you know? Well groomed but shifty-eyed? Like when you look at him he's staring at the haberdashery but you are absolutely convinced he's been watching your every move? Getting ready to pounce."

Catherine slams a tray of coffee cups on the counter and gives me a baleful look. "Just where did you learn about store detectives?" she demands.

Well. I don't know exactly. Have I displayed criminal intimacy? But Catherine is not really interested. Before I can get my defenses together, she launches a flank attack. "And another thing. I'm getting just a little tired of your witty remarks about other people's appearance."

"Well, I'm so sorry. I didn't know he was a special buddy or something."

"He is not a special buddy. I just think this adolescent . . . this adolescent . . ." She searches for the right word. Habit? ". . . habit should be curbed. Do you understand?"

Chastened but thoughtful, I am left alone in the kitchen to watch the water boil in the espresso pot. That really was an awful blunder, mistaking Mrs. Merkie for the professor's wife. How could I do such a thing? How old is he, anyway? The figure 102 leaps immediately to mind, but that can't be right. He looks sort of ageless, really. It's hard to imagine what he must have been like when he was little. I picture him going off to kindergarten in his neat blue suit. Fully formed, but smaller, and with a mighty shout. I wonder, too, if he could possibly be right about Mr. Barker. About his going into decline, corrupted by early success. It would be sad to think that the crumpled watercolors in the box were it. The peak. The best things he would ever do.

I open the white cardboard box from the bakery and peer at the four tarts inside. Sweet and gooey, glittering with sugar . . . Of course, Professor Merkie is probably wrong. He's wrong about Rothko, isn't he? If Mr. Barker had heard him, he would have been amused. "Ho, ho, ho," he would have said as his sad, knowing eyes scanned the room. They discover *Test Patterns*, a few odd sketches strewn about, and they fill with wonder. "Yours?" he asks. "Oh, just a few poor things," I say. He cannot believe it. Words fail him, but joy is in his glance as he reaches out his hand . . .

"Celine?" Catherine calls. "Could you bring in those tarts, after all? We've decided to sin."

I shiver back into reality and discover that there's only one tart left in the box. Panic wells up in my throat. It's a frame-up, obviously, but who will believe it?

SEVEN /

Thursday evening I am off to have supper with Lucile's family. What will happen, I wonder, in those tall buildings by the lake, when the electricity stops.

Nothing will work. Not the elevators or the intercoms, the televisions or the radios. Not even the toilets, I suspect. There are emergency lights in the stairwells, with powerful batteries in gray metal boxes, where people might gather and speculate. Not even these will last very long.

The people will have to go out eventually, but most will come back, feeling their way up dark stairs, counting each turn in the metal railings so that they will know when they reach their floor. The hallways will be difficult to navigate. Each door will feel very much the same. People may brush by each other in the dark, but no one will speak, because it will be so important not to lose count of the doors, which feel all very much the same. How relieved they will be when they find their own.

They will stand by their windows and look out over the dark city. It will be so quiet. Not a sound but that of someone occasionally brushing by in the hall or trying a key that doesn't fit. They will feel safe then.

Eventually, no one will go out at all.

Lucile's building is the tallest for miles around. The windows in the lobby are amber glass, and there is a doorman, who calls ahead to see if it is safe to let me inside. A little girl comes in with her mother while I'm waiting, and the doorman buzzes them in without a word. They are the good people who live inside. I wink at the little girl, but she only frowns. She understands that no one knows yet if I am a good person.

Lucile opens the apartment door for me. She is still in her bathrobe, damp and steamy. The bathrobe is not exactly clean, and the lapels are stained with makeup.

"Oh, God, Celine. You're early. Go talk to my sister while I get dressed."

She disappears, and I follow the sound of a television down a hall and into a large living room.

The set is not properly adjusted. The reds are intense, blooming into the other colors. A woman with greenish-blond hair is explaining how Jesus cured her drug addiction. As she moves her hands, her painted nails leave phosphorescent trails, like tracer bullets.

"You're Lucile's friend?" asks a girl sitting on a long white couch.

"Yes," I say, and then, because "friend" might be too strong a word, "we're in art class together."

The girl stands up and stretches so luxuriously that my eyes water. She must be Lucile's sister. She is older, skinnier, full of shadows. She would be pretty, but her face is puffy and thick-skinned, as if she's been sleeping for days.

"Yeah. Lucile is quite the little artist." She turns and looks at the television. The blond woman is holding hands with the evangelist. Their eyes are closed and they are praying for others to be cured of the curse of drug addiction. There is a *frisson* of sudden, barely suppressed excitement. An important message has just come in, by telepathy, it must be. The evangelist has detected someone in the viewing audience—a little boy named Ricky—who is suffering from a cleft palate and a spastic colon. He is at this moment being healed. At this very moment, praise God.

"I'm studying the sociology of religion at the University of Chicago," says the girl. "That's why I'm watching this."

I don't mind. I watch Christian broadcasting a lot myself. It's something about the men's hair. They have seamed and froggy faces, but extraordinary hair. I suspect it is their vanity. I picture them at their dressing tables, waiting for the show to go on, blow-dryer in hand. Do they have doubts? Do they wonder if it's wrong to have such beautiful hair? Are they tormented by the desires of the scalp?

"It's interesting," I say.

"You think so?"

"Well. Yes. Don't you?"

"Yeah, but then I'm not an artist."

The blond woman is inviting people who have just been healed to call up and share their experiences. Behind her are banks of grandmothers and grandfathers hunched over ringing phones. A number flashes on the screen.

"I used to be interested in art. I was pretty good, as a matter of fact. Maybe that was my problem. It was all too easy. You know what I mean? I kept asking myself, what's the point? Even if you're another Leonardo da Vinci, what's the point? Do you ever ask yourself that?"

"No," I say promptly.

The girl nods. She's not surprised. Her head is heavy with the wisdom she has picked up down at U of C.

"You probably will, when you're more mature. I mean, there are all these people starving in the world and getting raped. People getting raped and most of them not even knowing that they're getting raped . . ."

"Not knowing? Really? What do you mean?"

"Date rape. *You* know."

I do? This conversation is beginning to make me a little uncomfortable.

"So, anyway, I gave it up. You think this ashtray's pretty?" It is blue. Lumpy with pink valentine hearts.

"Beautiful."

"You think so? I made it."

"No, it's really nice."

"You can have it, then. I no longer value material (109) things." She pushes the ashtray into my hands. "You can have this, too. And this." She begins to move hurriedly around the room, picking up stuff and loading it into my arms. A *New Yorker* magazine with a Sempé cover, a glass paperweight with a rose inside, a framed picture of a woman with either a hat or a chicken sitting on her head, a box of lavender matches twelve inches long.

"You know . . ." She stops and regards me suspiciously. "I'm giving you all this stuff, and I don't even know your name."

"Celine." I extend one hand as far as I am able. Like a flipper. "I don't know yours, either."

"I am become death, destroyer of worlds."

Death and I shake hands. On the television the evangelist reports that a woman in Elmhurst has been healed of shingles.

I'm relieved when a tall, slender woman comes rapidly into the room.

"Really, Beth. There's no need to live in the dark." She twitches back the drapes impatiently and turns off the television before she looks at me. It must be Lucile's mother. She looks like Lucile, only tougher, more refined. No baby fat.

"You must be Celine." Her eyes fasten on the pile of her possessions that I'm holding in my arms. She smiles politely. She's sure there is some perfectly reasonable explanation. She will wait.

"Celine was going to show me how to juggle," says Beth. "Like the Brothers Karamazov on television."

"Oh? Don't jugglers use things like Indian clubs and hoops?" says Mrs. Higgenbottom, rescuing the portrait of the woman with the chicken on her head and replacing it on a glass bookcase. She steps back to look at it, and then adjusts its position fractionally.

"Not the Brothers Karamazov," Beth insists stoutly. "They juggle all sorts of things. Knives, telephones . . . I saw them juggle a cow's liver once."

"I don't really know how to juggle," I confess to Mrs. Higgenbottom.

"Then you should practice first with beanbags," says Beth severely. Her mother says nothing at all, but sniffs and touches her perfect hair.

For supper we are fed Cornish hens by a woman in a black dress and a white apron. Dear dead little birds. Ordinarily I have trouble eating adorable things, but I'm very much on my best behavior because I want to make a good impression on Lucile's parents.

Her father joins us. He doesn't say much, but I respect him because he refuses to pull the end of his tie out of his waistband when he sits down. He reports that it's out of harm's way there, and there it stays, stretched over his round tummy, secured from wandering into the gravy or being tossed with the salad.

We sit around a large polished table of rosewood, each of us isolated, but anchored to placemats of coarse linen. Mrs. Higgenbottom asks me questions about my family. She listens intently to everything I say. Such attention (111) keeps me, not honest exactly, but compliant. I'm ready to confess to anything.

"Lucile says you plan to be an artist," she concludes, fingering a stick of celery as if to gauge its crispness.

"Yes."

"I suppose you'll go to art school, then," says Mr. Higgenbottom, chewing thoughtfully.

"Well, yes. Sometime. Maybe in Italy."

"I don't suppose . . ." He frowns to show that in these matters he's willing to be instructed. "You get a degree in art or something like that. Is that right?"

"Yes. In painting or . . ." Something like that.

"What exactly do you do with a degree in art?" He looks at me wide-eyed over the gravy boat. I'm not to misunderstand. He's sure that there's some perfectly proper thing that you do. Probably, his look suggests, it would be obvious to anyone but a plain old commodity broker like him.

"Well . . ."

"Daddy!" says Beth, who's been silent. "You don't *do* anything with a degree in art. She's going to be an artist. What's wrong with that?"

Nothing. Nothing at all. Takes all sorts.

"You think she's going to starve or something? She'll probably be rich. She'll probably be in *People* magazine."

"If . . ." Mr. Higgenbottom raises his knife like a baton to make his point. "If she's got the talent."

"Daddy! You are so naïve. You think it takes talent? Do you think her stuff has to be any good? She just has to meet the right people, get the right line together. *She* knows that. She'll con their pants off."

"In the meantime," Mrs. Higgenbottom interrupts, "she might find it useful to have some salable skills. A young woman should have something to fall back on."

"She could teach," suggests Lucile. "Or illustrate kids' books."

Beth throws down her napkin in outrage on my behalf. "She can't do that! She can't plan to have something to fall back on. An artist has to take risks. If she has something to fall back on, then that's what she'll do. Fall back. Sometimes you people are so dense!"

"Now, that's enough of that, young lady," says her father. "It's planning that puts food on the table here."

"Why are you always talking about food? Throwing it up to me? I never get a moment's peace here! Never a moment!" Beth flees the table. Her father catches her chair with a practiced gesture as it overturns, and her mother looks at me reproachfully. I am to see what all this loose talk about art leads to.

After we have eaten, Lucile carries me off to her room. Her bed has turned posts painted white and gold and is crowded with stuffed animals.

"Are you really going to wear that skirt tonight? Didn't

you bring anything else?" she asks, her eyes wide with alarm.

"What do you mean? You said wear a dress. It's the only dress I've got."

"I know, but we might get invited to a party. You can't wear that to a party. You look like you stole it off a Girl Scout."

I suppose she's right. Still, I feel resentful. "It's all I've got," I insist. "What difference does it make, anyway?"

Lucile doesn't bother to explain. Indeed, she doesn't have to. The dope in me rises in protest. You can't go to a party looking like a Girl Scout, it says.

I sit on the bed and contemplate my knees while Lucile roots through drawers and in her closet.

"Put these on," she says, pushing a pair of pants into my hands. They are black and stretchy. They fit like long underwear. "And this." A bulky sweater with real shoulder pads. Blue-gray, with large geometric patterns in white and black.

She stands back and eyes me critically while I pull the sweater down over my tights as far as it will go.

"Huh," she says. I think she means it is hopeless. I'm afraid to look in the mirror. "You want to try some makeup? Can I make you up? I'm really good at it." I sit on the edge of the upholstered bench at her vanity table while she paints my face. As she puts in my eyes, her tongue draws circles around her lips. She is concentrating so hard that when our eyes meet, she doesn't even notice. For the artist, the eyes are simply another feature.

I have become invisible. All appearance. I think there is some irony here. I have been scheming to paint Lucile, and now she's painting me.

When she is finished, she wipes her nose with the back of her hand. She frowns, still very critical, but then, to my intense relief, she smiles.

"You know," she says, "you could be real cute."

I turn and look in the mirror. Great glittering gray eyes staring at me out of a pale face. It is true. Maybe I am not real, but I am cute. I had not known it would come to this. I have never wanted to be cute. Sophisticated, exotic, maybe. Never cute. I tell myself that I hate looking like this, and yet I feel it, the terrible temptation of cuteness.

"Look at Celine," Lucile says to Beth, who has wandered into the room, looking for worlds to destroy, no doubt. "Boy, Dermot is going to drop his teeth."

"Dermot? Is she going with Dermot Forbisher?"

"Yeah."

Beth surveys the transformed Celine with bitter contempt. "I wouldn't go with him," she says. "He is such a jerk."

I smile at her serenely in the mirror, secure in my cuteness. Behind me, Beth and Lucile begin to make arrangements about some party that they are both going to. It has nothing to do with me. I make faces at myself. I bat my eyes and try to look like a startled fawn, moistened lips slightly parted. Then I tuck my chin down, turn up the corners of my mouth, and close and open my eyes very slowly. The effect is truly amazing. So innocent,

yet daring. Is it true, I wonder. Has my life been transformed by Maybelline?

In the elevator on our way to meet Philip and Dermot,
Lucile and I are reflected an infinite number of times by
the mirrors in the walls. Our beauty and cuteness are
breathtaking. I arrange my sweater so that it isn't pulled
down quite so far and do a small bump and grind.

(115)

"Cool it," says the veteran Lucile indulgently. I try to
become serious then, but it is difficult. I'm prepared to
ride up and down the elevator all evening, admiring this
miracle of modern cosmetic technology. It can't be done.
I turn what's left of my mind to other matters.

"Why does Beth think that Dermot is a jerk?" I ask. I
can think of many reasons, but I'm curious to know what
part of his personality has caught her attention.

"She doesn't think he's a jerk. Not really. She has a
thing for Dermot."

"But she's in college." How could a person in college
have a thing for Dermot?

"So?" Lucile grins at me. "Maybe she likes them
young."

"I don't know." It still seems unnatural to me. "Is she
okay? She seems sort of weird."

"Weird? Beth? What's weird about Beth?" She is not
offended, but vaguely surprised.

"Well, she told me she was death, destroyer of worlds."

"Oh, she says that to everybody. She got it out of some
book or something. She thinks it makes her sound cool.
She's a wimp, really."

This doesn't reassure me. I can picture death as a

wimp. Sort of fat and knock-kneed, with the heels of his shoes all worn down unevenly. He has infinite power, but he still isn't happy, because he's so unpopular.

The dance at the school is a good dance. A nice dance. It's in the gym; the white lights overhead drive the shadows up into the bleachers where the tough boys lounge, and the smell of fruit punch lies like velvet over the permanent taint of sweat and floor wax. Dust ground fine in a thousand basketball games drifts through the air and burns my nose. I could have a good time here. I could be happy in my new makeup, my borrowed finery.

A solemn boy in a lavender jacket whose shoulders are still molded by a coat hanger asks me if I would like to join the International Relations Club, if I would like to dance. We bounce into the center of the floor with abandon. He is more dignified than I am, but respects my attempts to remain airborne. Other dancers edge away to admire from a safe distance my white Hi-Tops, flailing like propellers. Mr. Carruthers waltzes by, an assistant dean in his arms. They smile at me, at the boy in the lavender jacket, even at Linda Jarlowski, ordinarily so morose, tortured by myopia, by French conjugations. Tonight she has left her thick glasses at home. She can barely see her crowd of admirers, but still she *knows*. She dances carefully, mindful of tables, treacherous folding chairs, her round face dazed with happiness.

Up on the bandstand, Cory Sok, the smartest kid in the school, is playing bass. He knows all the moves.

Where did he learn? In what secret recesses of the heart did he find room to practice? I have seen him outside his father's grocery store, arranging red apples, downy peaches cushioned in tissue. I thought all his dreams were of refugee camps, blossoms of napalm, Cal Tech. I gape at him for ten minutes before he finally acknowledges the compliment with a slight grin, a toss up of black hair trained reluctantly to fall over his eyes.

"Do you need a road manager?" I shout above the noise.

"Huh?"

"I said, do you want to get married?"

Cory looks confused and misses a beat for the first time, but I never learn if my offer is to be accepted, my life reshaped in a single instant of passion. Dermot appears and drags me away.

"Stop clowning around, Celine," he says. "We're splitting." He looks indescribably weary and sophisticated in his new Italian jacket, white on white.

"What do you mean? We just got here."

"We're going to another party. A *real* party."

"This is a real party. I want to stay here and dance."

Lucile, draped boneless over a fire extinguisher near the door, rolls her eyes in disgust. "That's dancing? Whatever it is, Celine, it is not dancing."

I turn sullen at this remark, but it does me no good. Philip and Dermot are hustling me out into the night like a couple of KGB agents. "Are we really going to take her?" whispers Philip.

"Shut up," says Lucile loyally. "She's got to come. I promised my mom. Are you okay, Celine? You're acting kind of weird."

"Of course I'm okay. But what about your mother? Did you tell her about this other party?"

"Be real, Celine. It's just another party. Some of Beth's friends. Are you coming or not?"

"I don't want to go. I don't want to be real," I try to explain. They are remorseless and not interested.

We take a cab because it has begun to rain. A cold, appropriate drizzle. I sit in front next to the driver, watching drops of water creep away from the wiper blades on the windshield.

The driver is unhappy with the address that Dermot gives him. "You sure you kids want to go there?" he asks. "That is a very transitional neighborhood."

Dermot is fascinated. "No kidding? Pretty bad, is it?" He coaxes horror stories from the man. He is good at this. Tales of babies born in the backseat, hookers slicing up a john with razors in absolute silence, crack-mad muggers and decapitating accidents.

"No kidding?" says Dermot.

EIGHT /

The cab leaves us in front of one of those tall old buildings south of the Loop. It is dark and gloomy, shackled by rusty fire escapes, brooding over memories of child labor, girls in white shirtwaists poised to jump as flames lick over the oily floors behind them. People live here now, I am to believe. There is a small modern foyer of chrome and aqua tile. We crowd in together and Dermot studies the panel of name cards and doorbells.

"What's their name?" he asks after a minute.

"I can't remember," says Lucile. "Holzheimer or Holt-meyer or something like that."

"There's a Harry Frederick," says Dermot. "Does that sound like it?"

"Yeah, that must be it."

"What?" I protest. "Frederick isn't like Holzheimer."

"There isn't any Holzheimer," says Dermot and presses
the button firmly. We are buzzed through the security
door without a word. Expected we must be, by these
people whose name we don't know. I let Dermot navigate
me into the elevator, up many stories. We can hear the
party as soon as the elevator stops.

"Yeah, this must be it," Dermot says serenely.

The party is a large one, spilling a small crowd out
into the hall.

"Is this the Fredericks'?" we ask as we edge past. "The
Holzheimers'?" People smile and nod. Urge us forward
into a large room crowded with people eating and talking.
There is loud music, and the crowd sucks and surges like
the tide.

"Let's get out of here," I shout at Dermot. "We don't
know anybody here."

"Yeah, just a minute," he says, already being swept
away. I look around for Lucile, but she has disappeared,
too, and I am distracted by a sudden blunt poke against
my leg. I look down and see a dark German shepherd
watching me with crazy, smoky eyes.

"Don't look at him," advises a man edging past with
a large green bottle, splashing wine here and there.

"Who?"

"The dog. Don't let him catch your eye. He attacks if
he catches your eye."

"Why does he do that?"

"Because he feels *challenged*. It's this terrible burden of human expectations. He can't stand it. So he attacks, you see." The man stares moodily into his bottle. "That's what his analyst says, anyway. I suppose it makes sense. Does that make sense to you?"

I feel another hard poke and squeeze my eyes shut so I won't be challenging. "Yeah. I guess."

"Well, that's very understanding of you," says the man, nodding benignly. "Very understanding. His name is Wotan, by the way. Who are you?"

"Celine. Celine Morienval. I'm a friend of Beth Higgenbottom."

"Who you say? Death?"

"No. Beth."

"Never heard of her," says the man, rising up on his toes and trying to see over the crowd. "In fact, I don't recognize a single person at this party. I wonder if I'm in the right place. Whose party is it? Do you know?"

"Somebody named Harry Frederick, I think."

The man stares at me blankly. "I'm Harry Frederick," he says abruptly.

"Oh," I say. "I'm sorry. I didn't realize . . ."

The man gives me a reassuring smile. "Don't give it another thought, sport. Do you mind legs?"

"Excuse me?"

"I said, do you mind dregs?" He holds up his bottle. "It's all I've got left."

"Oh. No, thank you. I don't want anything to drink."

"Or maybe you'd like a tickle."

"What?"

"I said, would you like a pickle?" A dish of olives and pickled mushrooms appear in his other hand.

"Oh. No, thank you. If you don't mind, I think . . ."

Mr. Frederick looks puzzled. "You stink?"

"I think!" I bellow at him, as a man and a woman push between us with wild cries of delight. As they embrace I catch a glimpse of Mr. Frederick swept back into the crowd, nodding and smiling, mouthing words I happily can't hear at all.

Wotan pokes me again higher up, in the small of my back.

"Good dog," I say, fixing my eyes on the ceiling.

"Do you want something or don't you?" he says, and pokes me again. I turn and find he has been transmogrified into a small girl in a pale silk dress. She holds up a tray loaded with frayed canapés—pink sausages impaled on toothpicks, slivers of pastry with greenish slices of egg, gray liver-sausage, sweaty cheese.

"Thank you," I say, reaching for a sausage.

"Ick," she says, but without much expression. A good hostess, she doesn't want to influence my choice.

"What about these?" I ask, poking at a smoked oyster with a toothpick.

"They made Mrs. Ambrose sick," says the girl.

"Oh. Well, maybe I won't have anything."

"I wouldn't," she says and yawns hugely. We survey her tray of inedibles in companionable silence. I feel a certain affinity growing between us, and might ask her name, but a horde of hungry guests suddenly descends upon her and carries her away, tray and all. "Oh, you little doll!" shrieks a woman in a black hat with a shiny forehead. She looks absolutely ravenous and pinches the little girl's arm as if to test its meatiness. "I could eat you up," she cries. I might intervene, try to save her, but I'm set abruptly into motion myself by another hard poke in the rear. I'm sure it's Wotan this time. I stumble off through the crowd, feigning blindness, searching for Dermot and a way home. (123)

I find him in a corner beneath a potted palm having an intense conversation with Beth.

"You are such a jerk, Dermot," she is saying. He is deeply interested, straining to see through her eyes and into her head. Her shoulders are bare; every bone, every tiny muscle shows. The effect is one of complete nakedness. "You are such an idiot that I sometimes wonder how you find your way to school every day," she says.

Dermot flushes at this abuse, and I have to practically punch him to get his attention.

"Dermot," I say, "I want to go home now."

"What?" He risks a quick glance away from Beth's face, but even then I'm not sure he recognizes me.

"I want to go home. There's this dog who keeps trying to catch my eye."

"What? Who?" says Dermot.

"Wotan. His name is Wotan. I don't know where he is now, but he wants to bite me and I want to go home."

Beth's nostrils flare with contempt; her thin lips curl

like metal shavings spun off a lathe. "Yes. Really, Dermot. You should take the little thing home. I'm sure it's way past her bedtime."

"In a minute," says Dermot. He gives his head a shake to restore internal activity. "We just got here."

"Yes, Celine," says Lucile, leaning over my shoulder. She holds a wineglass with something pink inside. "Don't be so wet." She smiles lazily. "Is he nice?"

"Who?"

"Wotan or what's-his-name. Does he really bite?"

"He's a dog, you dope!"

"Woof," sighs Lucile dreamily, and I find myself carried away again by an eddy of revelers, washing up finally against a long table draped with a white cloth and covered with food. None of it looks very good. A savaged ham has slithered off its platter and cozied up to the corpse of a chicken. Someone has been using the clam dip as an ashtray, and a lady's wet slipper is resting in the corn chips. The guacamole looks halfway decent and I am about to console myself with a crackerful when I notice that the cracker says "Milk-Bone."

A familiar feeling of desolation comes over me. I'm very tired. This is not the life I wanted. I feel a great desire to get off the bus and wait in the deserted shelter for the next. When I was little and felt this way at a party, I would lie down on the floor. The first time I did it was at a restaurant in London where my father and mother and all my relations had gathered to decide who was going to get what child for the summer. I was six and feeling very grownup because I had a new dress with puff sleeves and I'd just had my hair cut and could feel my ears sticking out, but suddenly it seemed very alarming to me that my ears should be sticking out this way and I looked around the table at all the women there and they were all very beautiful without exception, but their ears didn't stick out. Worse, I wasn't sure which of them was my real mother anymore. Well, I did know, really, but I began suddenly to have these doubts. I'd lived with them all at one time or another, and what if I'd gotten mixed up? This idea was so scary that the only thing I could think of was to lie down on the floor. No one seemed to mind, but then a waiter asked whose child is this and the most beautiful woman leaned down and hissed at me to get under the table. That must be my real mother, I thought, and crawled under the table and lay down with my head on my father's shoes. I was very content then, my hands folded on my stomach, looking up my mother's dress and admiring her beautiful white underclothes . . .

I look thoughtfully at the tablecloth hanging to the floor, but of course it isn't possible to escape that way anymore. That is the great problem with maturity. One's escape routes become fewer and fewer.

I shuffle into the kitchen, looking for the back door or the trash compactor. There must be some way out of here.

I find the back door easily enough, manipulate a variety of chains and bolts, but it still refuses to open.

"You have to have a key," says a small, still voice that

makes me jump. It's the little girl, wearing a large white apron over her silk dress now, and sitting on a stool in the narrow space between the refrigerator and the wall.

She smiles at me wanly. "If you want to leave, you have to go through there." She leans forward and peers around the refrigerator at the doorway through which I have just come. It seems to bulge with people and hilarity. A permanent blockage.

"Oh. Maybe I'll just stay here for a while. Are you okay?" I ask because she looks so wan and frail sitting there in her white apron. Her hair is the color of potato sprouts; her eyes are rimmed with pink.

"Yes. I'm just resting."

"Maybe you should go to bed."

She shrugs. "I can't yet. There're some people in my room, and anyway I'm in charge of the food. I have to make some more pâté right now, as a matter of fact." She gets up wearily and goes to the kitchen table.

"Do you want me to help?" I ask hopefully. She's so calm and dignified. I think I will spend the rest of the evening with her.

"That would be nice, actually," she says. "Actually, I feel run absolutely ragged. Here. You can make some seafood dip." She presses a can of cat food and a jar of mayonnaise into my hand. She herself scrapes out the contents of a can of Mighty Dog and begins to mash them in a bowl with an avocado.

"That looks good," I say.

"Yes. I'm told it tastes like *terrine à lapin*," she says. "I haven't tried it myself, of course."

"No. Of course not. Doesn't Wotan mind?"

"Oh, no. He's a very generous dog. As long as you don't look in his eyes. Anyway, there isn't anything else to eat now. I don't know why that is. No matter how much food Daddy buys, there's never enough. Isn't that a puzzle?"

"Yes, it certainly is. How does this look?" I say, exhibiting my seafood dip.

The girl frowns over it critically, but I am not offended. I realize I'm in the presence of genius.

"Well," she says, "it looks a bit green. Why don't you add a little Tabasco? A lot of Tabasco, as a matter of fact."

"Like this?"

"Yes. That looks delicious. What's your name?"

"Celine."

"We'll call it mixed seafood à la Celine, then."

"Thank you," I say. We smile at one another. Small islands of sanity in a darkling plain where ignorant armies clash by night.

I am just about to take out a bowl of Kibbles 'n Bits to replace the bowl of corn chips with their garnish of shoe, when Philip waylays me.

"Celine? I've been looking all over for you. Something's the matter with Lucile. You've got to help her."

"What? What's the matter with Lucile?"

"I don't know. She's locked herself in the bathroom and she's crying." I feel my fragile peace cracking, beginning to crumble. I turn to the little girl, hoping she can save me, but she simply raises her hands, her eyebrows. What can one do? she seems to ask. I am cast adrift. Philip takes me by the elbows and pilots me out into the crowd.

"What's wrong?" I ask him again.

"I don't know, I don't know. She's crying and won't open the door." He's really upset, which I am glad to see, but it's worrisome, too. What an awful place this is. I feel exactly like the rubber bumpers on the front of a tugboat as Philip pushes me through the dancers to the bathroom. Everything seems noisier and wilder. The air is rank with the smell of queer smoke, sweat, mysterious chemicals, alcohol and perfume. I think if we don't get out of here soon the whole place will spontaneously explode. Perhaps it's only the lack of oxygen which keeps us safe.

There are a number of people gathered in the corridor outside Lucile's bathroom, trying the handle, kicking the door gently.

"Is that your friend in there?" asks the lady with the black hat.

"Yes. Is she okay?"

"How should I know? Would you just get her out of there? Do you mind?"

Do I mind? I don't know. I really don't know what I'm doing here at all, but rather than try to explain to the lady in the black hat, I just knock on the door. "Lucile? Open up. It's me. Celine."

Nothing happens.

"Where's Beth?" I whisper to Philip.

He swallows. "She's busy," he says, apparently to

someone hovering six inches over my head. "She and Dermot . . . They're busy."

"What do you mean, busy? Where?"

"In the maid's room, I think it is. But I don't think we should bother them right now. They're, uh, busy."

We are looking into one another's troubled eyes and considering the implications of this when I hear a small voice from the other side of the door. "Celine?"

"Yes. Yes, it's me, Lucile. What's wrong? Open the door."

"Just you come in, Celine. Okay?"

"Okay."

I hear her fumble with the lock for a moment, then there's silence and I open the door.

I don't see what's wrong at first. Lucile is sitting on the floor in the small space between the toilet and the tub and looking up at me with the eyes of someone waiting for the rubber truncheons and electric shocks. There's a bad smell, but nothing else. No obvious mess.

"I'm sick," she whispers.

I go in, flicking on fans, trying to open a window that doesn't open, turning on a red heat lamp in the ceiling by mistake, so that the temperature immediately begins to soar. Philip and the lady with the black hat are staring at Lucile with the blank faces you see around traffic accidents. I kick the door closed.

"What's wrong? Are you going to throw up?" I find a washcloth and run some cold water on it and mop at her scared little face.

"I already did," she says, her face crumpling.

"Well, that's okay. You didn't take any pills or anything, did you? Let's just get out of here." I try to pull her up, but she resists, hugging herself tightly.

"I can't. I can't. What am I going to do?"

"It's all right. Really, it is. Lots of people throw up for all sorts of reasons. We'll just go home. Okay? We won't even say thank you and goodbye."

"No. No-o-o-o. You don't understand. I threw up . . ." She adds something in a whisper that I can't quite hear.

"What?" The room shudders, as if there had been a barely noticed earthquake. "What did you do?"

"There were all these people. I didn't know what to do." She plucks at her sweater with hands that are shaking so much they have no strength left, and I suddenly understand. She has thrown up inside her own sweater.

"Oh, Lucile. You dumb thing. You dumb, dumb thing." I'm shaking now almost as much as she is. I'm sorry for her, but even more, I'm terrified. This is it, I think. This is the price you have to pay to be Lucile Higgenbottom, the most beautiful girl in the world. You have to throw up inside your own clothes. I don't know what to do. How can anyone help her? I kiss her a couple of times on her eyes all streaming with tears and mascara and then try to be practical. I'm still hysterical, and the best thing I can think of is to shove her into the shower, clothes and all. She lifts her beautiful face to the cold needles of water, and it is truly awful then, her makeup streaking into mask and her bright hair matting as a mess of punch and clam dip runs out of her sweater and over her slacks and shoes.

"Oh! Oh! Oh!" I moan, trying to help her, running to the door in a panic to escape, and then running back and pulling at her sweater.

"Oh! Oh! Oh!" she moans in response, and then we moan "Oh! Oh! Oh!" together in counterpoint until Philip starts pounding on the door again and demanding to know what's wrong.

I pull the shower curtain, take a deep breath, and go to reassure him.

"Everything's okay," I say, and pretending to be in control does calm me down. "Go find some clean clothes. A sweat suit or something."

"Where?"

"I don't know. There must be closets full of stuff around here."

"But I don't know whose place this is!"

"Then it's time you got introduced," I say, and close the door again.

By this time, Lucile has gotten out of most of her clothes. I help her with the rest and then give her some soap and try to wring out her clothes as best I can in the toilet. What a nutty thing, I keep telling myself. That's all it is. Just another nutty thing. When I give Lucile a clean towel, she clutches my shoulder and whispers in my ear. "Celine? I want to die, Celine."

"Shut up. Shut up, Lucile. You're drunk. Look what Philip found you. A sweat suit. An Oscar de la Renta sweat suit." I display the lovely outfit which Philip has just slipped through the door as furtively as if it were the plans for the MX missile.

"Oh, yeah. Philip. I don't like him anymore, Celine."
She turns very solemn. "He can't control himself."

"You can't either, you dummox." I cram her into the sweat suit. "Let's go. We'll get a cab."

"Just a minute," says Lucile, and brushes her teeth with a finger and toothpaste. "Okay," she says. "I'm ready."

And she is ready. Her face is calm and dignified. There will be no questions. A glance will crush the raised eyebrows. No one, none of you, will ever be this beautiful.

NINE /

It is late when I get home. The forty-watt bulbs in the stairwell are particularly dim and futile. They cast their pallid glow over the broken tiles, the paths worn in the dust by feet, mine among them, forever trudging up and down these stairs. Sometimes I don't think I'm ever going to get out of here. I hope Catherine will still be awake so I can tell her about the party. About Wotan and the marvelous little girl, and how I had a dip named after me and Lucile threw up in her sweater.

It's dark inside the loft. She must be asleep. I kick off my shoes and, because I'm suddenly very hungry, get a carton of fruit yogurt out of the refrigerator and start working my way down to the jam. I don't turn on the television, and in the silence I can hear Celine-Beast. She's crooning at me from her newsprint pad. "Hey, Celine," she whispers. "I could be really nice to you. Come on over and check me out."

I resist. I know better. If she looks good, then I'll have to start working on her some more, and tomorrow is, after all, a school day. If she looks bad . . . Well, that isn't possible, is it? No, of course not. But of course I do have to walk right by her on my way to the bathroom. A glance would be natural enough. What am I supposed to do? Close my eyes every time I walk by a picture of mine? That wouldn't be very professional.

I flip back the cover of the pad, and she isn't there. Somebody, some ignorant vandal, has been messing in my charcoal, I tell myself. But it isn't so. It's worse than I could possibly have imagined. I've destroyed her. This isn't Celine-Beast. It's a rubbing of a manhole cover, the cardboard mattress of a bum on a hot-air grate.

"Is that you, Celine?" Catherine calls from her plasterboard room that Mel Hollingsford built in the back of the loft next to the bathroom.

"Yeah, it's me. Aren't you asleep?"

"I *was*. Are you okay? What are you moaning about?"

"Nothing. Ordinary, everyday despair."

Catherine's room is very small. The water bed practically fills it up. To get to the window, I have to trudge across her ankles. The bed quivers and shakes. I sit down on the windowsill.

"Catherine. Can I ask you a serious question? Do I have any talent?"

"Yes. You're marvelous. You're the greatest thing since Picasso. Okay? Now go to bed."

"You really think so? I mean, you don't have to spare my feelings or anything. Can I turn on the light?"

"No. Go to bed."

"I'm going. I really am." I fumble around for the string above her pillows and give it a tug. The cool fluorescent bulb in the wall flickers and one blue eye peers at me out of the tangle of her honey-colored hair. It is hard and gemlike. She's in one of her grumpy moods, I see. I'll have to cheer her up. One of my duties.

"Listen . . . You want me to get you a Coke or something?"

"No. I want to go back to sleep."

"Yeah, but this really strange thing happened tonight. You know my friend Lucile? She got sick and threw up, but she couldn't get to a toilet, so she threw up in her sweater. Isn't that terrible? What do you think it means?"

"It means she'll have a large dry-cleaning bill."

"Yeah, but . . ." I begin, and then I have a sudden very clear vision of the plastic bag of clothes sitting forlorn and forgotten in the back of the taxi. I must have noticed it. How else could I have such a clear picture? Oh, brother. What's her mother going to say? While I'm trying not to think about this, Catherine moans softly and throws out one arm along her pillows. She is wearing one of her sleazy white nightgowns and her bare shoulder is revealed. I can see every convolution of muscle and skin; my X-ray eye penetrates even to the bone, the cunning fit of knob and socket. So that's the way it is. How could I have forgotten?

"Hey. Could you hold that pose? Not move a muscle?"

"Get out of here, Celine. I'm really very, very tired."

"No, no," I say. "Just a minute. Let me get my sketchbook. You can even go to sleep if you want. I promise. I just want your shoulder, actually." As I'm about to gallop across the foot of the bed, Catherine sits up, tugging at the covers.

"Are you drunk, Celine? I . . . want . . . to . . . go . . . to . . . sleep! I have to get up early tomorrow. I'm going to a conference in Madison."

"A conference? What kind of conference?"

"Educational psychology. I'll be back Sunday night. Okay?"

"Yeah. I suppose. When did this come up?"

"Today. I mean, I knew about the conference before, but I didn't think I'd be able to go. Some friends have offered me a ride."

"Oh. Well, could I get my sketchbook? You can curl up and sleep like a baby. Really. I just want your shoulder. Could you hold your arm out like you were flying? Like you had a wing instead of an arm?"

"Celine! Go to bed!" Catherine flops over and turns out the light.

All right. All right for you. I can tell when I'm not wanted.

"And wash your face. You've got charcoal all over it."

"That's not charcoal. That's makeup. I'm beautiful!"

"You look like a little tart."

This is too much. "You're supposed to talk to me when (137) I get home from a party!" I yell at her, literally bouncing out of the room off the water bed, throwing my clothes hither and yon. "You're supposed to take an interest in my maturation processes!"

I grumble my way into the bathroom and wash all my cuteness down the drain. While I'm brushing my teeth, I discover another grievance, and stick my head in the door of her room. "Now I'm upset and won't be able to sleep, and I have school tomorrow!" I tell her, overwhelmed by the thought of a night spent tossing and turning on my overheated sheets. It brings tears to my eyes.

"Take your toothbrush out of your mouth when you talk."

"Just you wait. I'm going to tell Dad about how you neglect me when I can't sleep!" I yell, climbing into my bed. "You're not nice to me! You're not nice at all." I throw myself onto my futon and twist my pillow into an uncomfortable knot. She'll be sorry when she wakes up and finds me dead of exhaustion. "Forgive me, Celine," she'll say, gathering my lifeless but still attractive body into her arms. To stay awake, I try to concentrate on the little girl all serene and ethereal in her silk dress, but somehow my mind veers sharply to a disturbing image of Dermot and Beth in the maid's room. Those long, skinny arms like flexible cable wrapped around his bulk. Ah! Sweet mystery of life! By which I mean sex. I'm beginning at last to understand those darker, irrational impulses that shape one's life. I know these urges. Haven't I borne the weight of a work glove upon my knee in numb tranquillity? And not only that. I have yielded in other ways. I, too, have done strange and inexplicable things, almost against my will. I've cut off all my eyebrows with embroidery scissors, poked holes in the wallpaper where it wrapped around the corner by my bed, even pushed a navy bean up my nose. I remember very clearly sitting at the kitchen table, fingering the small white bean and savoring the solemnity of the moment just before I pushed it, irrevocably it seemed, up my left nostril. Yes, I know what it is for the body to be invaded by foreign objects, half consented to.

But there is one thing I have never understood. The central mystery of sex. And that is: How does it ever finally happen? I used to wonder at the movies. Here would be this man and this woman being chased by the Nazis, and in the next scene they're making love, with the Gestapo practically on the doorstep. How does it connect? What has this to do with the plot? With life? How did it come up in the conversation? It defies imagination. My imagination, anyway. Take Dermot and Beth, for example. When I left them, they seemed to be making plans to avoid each other for the rest of their lives, but somehow, while I was off in the kitchen making hors d'oeuvres, they managed to steer the conversation around to . . .

what? Why is it that their conversational skills are so much better than mine?

Catherine wakes me up in the morning, tugging back the drapes from the studio windows in her brisk and brutal way. The curtain rings scrape along the rod; my backbone curls in sympathy.

"Wake up, Celine," she says. "You're going to be late for school."

I consider this possibility for a moment, making little experiments with my eyelids to see if they are still in working order. They feel queer, as if they were made out of eggshells. The room is filled with suffocating light. I can hear Catherine moving quietly about the loft, flushing toilets, slamming books against the wall, strangling the cat . . .

"There isn't any school today," I yell at the ceiling. "It's senior cut day."

"Senior what?" says Catherine in an ordinary voice. She has returned and is standing underneath my bed, fiddling with the tea caddy, where we keep the household cash.

"You know. Senior cut day. Seniors are supposed to cut. I'd look like an idiot if I went to school today."

"But you're not a senior."

"Well, I know I'm not a senior technically, but I have enough credits to graduate, so I am a senior—technically speaking." Catherine looks simply baffled. She has no mind at all for technical discussions.

"What I mean is . . ." I begin again patiently, but she isn't listening.

"Listen," she says, "you are going to school today. That's final. I'm leaving fifty . . . Stop making those peculiar faces, Celine. Do I have your attention? Your full attention? Then listen. I'm leaving fifty dollars in the tea caddy. That should be more than you could possibly need. Just because it's there doesn't mean you have to spend it all."

"Where are you going?"

"I told you. Last night. I'm going to a conference in Madison for the weekend. I'll be staying in the Alumni Center. The number is on the bulletin board. In case of dire emergency, you can call the Frankels or Professor Kimball. Jean Barker would help you out, too, but I haven't been able to get hold of her. Do you think you can manage?"

Of course I can manage. There is even some reason why it's very nice for Catherine to go away for the weekend. It's trying very hard to edge into my consciousness.

"I'm sorry that there isn't much in the house to eat. This came up on such short notice. You can order a pizza tonight if you want. Tomorrow you can go over to the Frankels'."

"No. That's okay. Tomorrow I'm going to . . ." I become fully conscious just in time and stifle revelation with a yawn.

"What are you going to do?" Catherine peers up at me suspiciously.

"Never mind."

"Never mind what?"

"What I was going to say."

"What were you going to say?" (141)

"When?" I settle down comfortably in the covers. I can go on like this for hours, but Catherine gives up immediately. I can hear her banging cupboard doors in the kitchen. It doesn't matter. I'm not really going to help Mr. Barker paint his studio. Whatever dumb things I might do in my life, that is not going to be one of them. I hop out of bed with that clean, clear feeling of having made the right decision.

Two minutes later I'm practically in tears because I can't find any clean underwear that doesn't come up to my armpits and have little blue flowers all over it. What will I wear to Mr. Barker's tomorrow? I mean, what if I had to take off my pants for some perfectly innocent reason? It would be utterly humiliating.

I remember once in science class when Miss Hobbs was showing us this movie about saving the poor birds who had been trapped in an oil spill. It was terrible. The poisonous oil covering their feathers, getting all over them, everywhere. I thought of Steve McQueen and how much I would like to work with him saving those poor birds and how I might fall into a puddle of the terrible oil myself, and there would be no time to lose; it must all be cleaned off at once with cotton puffs and cold cream, and how we must be brave and not be bothered by the fact that it had even gotten inside my clothes.

When I thought of Steve McQueen and me being brave together in this way I nearly fainted, right there in science class, and poor Miss Hobbs had to go to the principal's office and promise that she wouldn't show such terrifying movies to sensitive children anymore.

Of course, it isn't likely that there will be any oil spills at Mr. Barker's studio, but varnish remover, for instance. What if we're stripping the woodwork and . . . When I realize what's going through my head, I give a little scream and run into the bathroom and scrub my face with Noxzema. The fumes clear my head. Tomorrow, I tell myself firmly, I will stay home and write my paper on Holden Caulfield. If I get hungry, I will order a pizza. Yes. Double cheese, with pepperoni and mushrooms.

On my way to the kitchen I wonder what Mr. Barker will feed me. Is it possible that I might persuade him to take me to the Thai Little Home Café? I love Thai food, but of course . . . What in heaven's name is the matter with me? I seemed to have been transformed into the girl with two brains. They don't even argue. They simply prattle along together, each confident that it's the one in charge.

The phone rings, and my two brains manage to co-ordinate a detour to pick it up. It is Mr. Barker, I hope and fear. I will tell him that I am sorry but my dance card is filled for the rest of my life. Yes, I will definitely tell him that it is the Thai Little Home Café or nothing.

"Hello?" I say, wondering what's going to come out next.

"This is Mrs. Bradford Higgenbottom. May I speak to
Mrs. Morienval?"

"Oh. Hi, Mrs. Higgenbottom. How's Lucile? This is
Celine."

"I know who this is. May I speak to your mother,
please?" She is so cool that the receiver turns to ice in
my hand, and I don't even explain that my mother is far
away and it would be a very expensive call, not that I
would object. Instead, I go to fetch Catherine, walking
on my toes so as not to disturb anyone else in the universe.
Mrs. Higgenbottom is angry about something. What
could it be? Nothing to do with me certainly. Didn't I
do everything right?

I find Catherine chopping up carrots and carving rad-
ishes into flowers. She chops with vigor. Perhaps it re-
lieves her feelings. On the counter beside her is an open
picnic hamper. The shapely legs of a roast chicken peek
out from a nest of waxed paper, kaiser rolls, snowy linen.

"It's for you," I say.

"Who is it?"

"Mrs. Bradford Higgenbottom."

"Who?"

"Lucile's mother."

"Who's Lucile?"

"You know. I told you about her. We went to that
party last night together."

"Why does she want to talk to me?"

"I don't know. How should I know?" I begin to relax.
I *don't* know. It's much easier to carry on a conversation

with Catherine if you can claim total ignorance. Still, I feel some unease when she throws down the knife and goes off to the phone. I see in her glance that she expects something awful. I decide to chop up a few carrots myself to see if it really does relieve feelings. There's a certain satisfaction, but I also chop my thumb and am busy bleeding when Catherine comes back.

"What exactly happened last night?" she says.

"To Lucile, you mean? I told you. She got sick."

"Mrs. Bradford Higgenbottom says she was smashed. Don't bleed on the chopping board."

I hold my hand over the sink and admit that it is possible that Lucile might have had too much to drink.

"Too much? *Any* is too much. And what happened to her clothes? Mrs. Higgenbottom says she lost all her clothes."

"Oh, yeah. We left them in the taxi, I think. She can get them back, probably."

"Don't bleed on the carrots. Why did she take her clothes off in a taxi? Is that what you're going to tell Mrs. Higgenbottom?"

"Me?" I bellow. "Why do I have to tell Mrs. Higgenbottom anything? It wasn't my fault!"

"Now, don't get hysterical, Celine. And stop bleeding all over the place."

"I can't stop bleeding! I've forgotten how to clot! Here you are, giving me the third degree, and I'm bleeding to death!"

Some measure of tranquillity is finally restored. While Catherine swathes my thumb in paper towels, she extracts an account of what happened at the party. It seems a strangely dreary one in the cold light of day—a useful object lesson about the disasters visited upon the muddleheaded. I should not have gone to the second party. I should have persuaded Lucile to respect the confidence of her mother. I should not have let her have anything to drink. I should have insisted that Dermot and Philip take us home immediately, and, if they refused, called a cab myself. I should not have put Lucile in the shower. That was very peculiar. And I should have accompanied Lucile to her door and then and there explained the situation to Mrs. Higgenbottom. "Then all this fuss would have been avoided," Catherine concludes brightly. "Just use your head next time."

I nod in dumb agreement, but the truth is, I feel discouraged. Not one of Catherine's suggestions had ever even occurred to me. And yet she's right. I should have done all those things. I should have, for example . . . My mind goes blank. What? Leapt tall buildings at a single bound?

Catherine seals up the carrots with a contented sigh. "There," she says. "I'm glad we had this little talk. Mrs. Higgenbottom seemed to think that everything was your fault, but I knew that couldn't be right. Why don't you call her up sometime this weekend when she's cooled down a bit, and explain?"

"Me?" I ask feebly.

"Well, that would be best, and since I won't be here . . ."

"Okay." I sigh. The choice seems clear enough. Is

Mrs. Higgenbottom going to destroy my reputation forever and make all sorts of trouble, or am I going to make this one simple phone call? I sigh doubly. I'd better start making my travel arrangements immediately.

"Don't eat those," says Catherine, slapping a roselike radish from my good hand. I make a halfhearted grab at a kaiser roll, but I can't have that, either.

"But I'm starving!" I complain, distraught at all this food being whisked away to Madison, Wisconsin.

"Then fix yourself some breakfast," hisses Catherine, jamming packages into her hamper to save them from the ravenous Celine.

"Can I have the carrots? The bloody ones?"

"Bloody hell!" says Catherine in sudden shock, and begins hurriedly to unpack the hamper. Her fears are justified. The carrots in their little Tupperware box are garnished with a few gouts of blood—a precious condiment. She holds them under the faucet, splashing water all over the kitchen.

"Why don't you just give them to me? What if there's a drop left? Do you want to turn your friends into cannibals?"

Catherine seals up the box and returns it to the hamper, but she is now hesitant and thoughtful.

"What if they accidently eat my blood? That would make them cannibals, wouldn't it?" I think I've got her. She sags against the sink and puts one trembling hand to her forehead.

"I think . . ." she says wistfully. "I think you would have to be dead first."

"Oh." This is an interesting idea. I consider it carefully while Catherine goes to finish dressing and I slice a few bananas into a bowl of cornflakes. I have just come to a conclusion when the doorbell rings.

(147)

"I don't think you can be right," I shout to Catherine as I go to answer it. "I mean, what if you just amputated a guy's leg and ate that? You'd be a cannibal, wouldn't you? Even if you just had a couple of bites? I mean, if he was still alive? What if . . ."

Professor T. Merkie stands before me in the doorway, rigid with astonishment in his neat blue suit.

"There you are, Ted," calls Catherine. She stands perfectly at ease near the bathroom door, adjusting an earring. The professor peers over me as if I were a table lamp.

"Hello," he says. "Shall I wait in the car? I'm double-parked."

"No, no," says Catherine. "Come in. I'll just be a minute."

The professor edges carefully into the room. Smiles thoughtfully at the sofa, frowns at the polished caps of his shoes.

As I watch him, all sorts of barely noticed details and peculiar circumstances are being juggled up out of the sediment of my brain. The sudden decision to go to Madison with unidentified friends, the lavish lunch, the shrimp curry, the unheard-of agreement about the fate of contemporary art . . . There is, possibly, a pattern here. A web of fragile threads. It is all very suspicious.

"Hurt your hand?" the professor asks.

"Yes."

"Not serious, I hope," he says hopefully.

I don't have time for chitchat. I follow Catherine into the bathroom, where I find her intent upon darkening her fair eyebrows. She blinks with satisfaction at her reflection in the mirror. I try to maneuver into her peripheral vision.

"Well! I must say," I say. "This seems just a little tacky to me. I mean, really. An educational psychology conference. At least you could have arranged to be kidnapped, like in As the World Turns."

"Hmm?" says Catherine, amused.

"Well, maybe it was The Young and the Restless. It was some soap. Anyway . . ."

"I don't have the faintest idea what you're talking about," says Catherine calmly through her nose. "I never have the faintest idea what you're talking about."

"You want to know what? What I'm talking about? Is that the what what you want to know? About?" Catherine's eyes meet mine in the mirror in innocent bewilderment. Am I really going to confront her with my suspicions? I can feel my jaw flapping up and down and we both wait patiently for something to come out.

"What I'm talking about is that I don't have any decent clothes, and I want you to take me shopping tomorrow. I don't even have any socks. I'm the only kid in the school without socks, and you said you'd take me shopping tomorrow."

"I said what?"

"Well, maybe you didn't say tomorrow, but you're always on to me about how I dress!"

"You never want to go shopping! Never once in six weeks! I've asked you and asked you, but you never . . ." (149)

"I want to go now! Tomorrow!"

Catherine begins to slap her makeup into her purse. "You're impossible, Celine. I'll take you shopping when I get back. Now I'm going to Madison."

She seems to mean it. She collects her suitcase from the bedroom and the picnic hamper from the kitchen. I dog her footsteps, writhing and pleading, while Professor Merkie performs slow pirouettes to stay out of our way.

"I mean it," I say in desperation. "If you go away, I might do something rash!"

Catherine stops in her tracks and looks at me curiously. "Rash? What are you talking about now?"

"I'm not telling. But it's rash. I need supervision. People my age need almost constant supervision. Everyone knows that. We're a mass of raging hormones. What's Dad going to say when he comes back and finds out that you went away and left me for the weekend?"

Professor Merkie pulls at his tie. "Really, Catherine," he begins. "I had no idea Celine was ill . . ."

"Your father," snaps Catherine. She means my father, not Professor Merkie's. "Your father seems to have forgotten that he even has a daughter. I've noticed it before. A convenient habit of his. But if he thinks that he can simply waltz away for a couple of months and leave me alone with . . ."

"With what?" I interrupt so she can't say it. "Go ahead. Say it!"

Catherine sits down abruptly on her suitcase, and I find myself staring at the top of her head. The neat clean part, the little bump where an errant cowlick has resisted a lifetime of brushing.

"I think you'd better go ahead without me, Ted. This doesn't seem to be a good time." She doesn't look at either of us. She glances around the room where she's been living for six weeks with no one to come home to but me. There are two new lines on either side of her nose. Her nostrils are pink and shiny. I'm suddenly so anxious to get her out of the house that I can hardly breathe.

"No. That's okay. I can manage."

If Catherine is surprised by this sudden reversal, she doesn't show it. She shakes her head sadly and removes a bit of fluff from her skirt.

"No, Celine. I don't understand what's happening, but you need me here, I suppose . . ."

"No. Seriously. I don't know what I was yelling about. I can't go shopping tomorrow, anyway. Lucile is coming over to have her portrait painted."

Catherine argues some more, quietly and pathetically, but we know how the conversation will end. It is simply a matter of completing the figures of the dance while restraining the impulse to bundle them bodily out into the street.

"Well, if you're really sure . . ." says Catherine. The

professor looks at his watch impatiently. "We should really get a move on, Catherine," he says. "Mother will be wondering what's happened."

Poor Catherine. Already on her feet, ready to find happiness, she freezes as she stoops for the picnic hamper.

"Mother?"

"Yes. Just one of those last-minute decisions. She doesn't really get out in the country enough." He urges Catherine to action with a little pat on her elbow. I'm afraid that she may simply topple forward on her nose, like the dynamited statue of the overthrown dictator, but she keeps her balance and wobbles into the hall. It's too complicated to turn back now.

"Bye-bye," I say, watching them go down the hall toward the stairs. I'm relieved to see that they are hugging opposite walls. It won't, I'm afraid, be much of a weekend after all, despite the educational psychology. I could have told her. About what a washout Merkie would be. All he can do is parody the aspirations of the past.

"Avoid the carrots," I call after him cheerfully. To show my heart is in the right place. I'm not understood. Perhaps Catherine is right and I am losing contact with reality. It doesn't seem much of a loss.

TEN /

I'm no more than twenty minutes late to school. I'm bustling through the empty halls, muttering nonsense under my breath so as to appear preoccupied and businesslike in case I'm spotted by a hall monitor, when Lucile lunges out of a janitor's closet and drags me inside.

"Where've you been?" she says. "I'm going to be late for chemistry now."

I'm all apologies, but curious as to why we're hanging out with the brooms.

"Listen," says Lucile. "We've got to get our stories straight about what happened last night."

"Oh, yeah. What did you tell your mother, anyway? She . . ."

"I told her that we just met some friends of yours on the way home from the school dance, and they sort of lured us into this other party. I thought I was drinking Cherry Coke. Remember that. Cherry Coke."

"*My* friends! What are you talking about? Those were Beth's friends."

"Don't mention Beth. Do not under any circumstances mention Beth. She and a friend spent the evening in the library doing research. But nobody will expect you to know that. So forget it. You don't know anything about Beth. And don't mention Philip."

"Oh. What was he doing?"

"I don't know yet. I haven't talked to him. I wanted to talk to you first, and you're late." She pouts reproachfully. She has a perfect attendance record and now I've ruined it.

"I said I was sorry. But listen, anyway . . ."

"And the reason I lost my clothes is that we went over to your house because I realized that somebody had spiked my Cherry Coke. You get it? We were embarrassed about it. And we spilled coffee on them. On my clothes. So all you have to do is get them cleaned and everything will be all right."

"Listen to me, Lucile. Your mom already called."

"What?" Lucile staggers around the closet and I have to practically climb in the sink to escape.

"What did you tell her? Does she know?"

"I didn't talk to her. My stepmother did. But anyway . . ."

"Then it's still okay, isn't it? You've got to help me,

Celine. I've already been grounded for the rest of the term. I don't know what she'll do if she finds out what really happened."

"But what about me?" I say, beginning to feel a little indignant. "If I tell some story like that, I'll get grounded, too!" I don't know why I say this. My father would be amazed to discover anything but airplanes could be grounded.

"But what difference would that make?" the despairing Lucile cries. "What if you do get grounded? You never do anything anyway."

There is a kind of fascinating logic to this argument, but it's pointless to pursue its dodges and turns.

"It doesn't matter, Lucile. I already told my stepmother."

Lucile shrinks away. "What? What did you tell her?"

"Well. Everything, more or less."

Lucile straightens her shoulders. Her face is calm. With the tip of her finger, she catches a drop of clear water forming on the lip of the janitor's faucet and examines it.

"Did you tell her about my getting sick? How I threw up?" she asks very quietly.

"Well, yeah. But listen, Lucile. If we just tell your mom the truth, it will be so much simpler. Don't . . ."

She isn't listening. She is watching my face with victim's eyes.

"How could you do that?" she whispers. "Now everyone will know."

"Know what? That you threw up in your sweater? But that's not a bad thing. And nobody is going to . . ."

"Don't touch me!" We both stare at my grubby, grasping hand until it withers.

There doesn't seem to be anything more to say. Lucile opens the door and then looks at me over her shoulder. "You've ruined my life," she says with breathless amazement. And then she's gone.

I sit down on a five-gallon drum of floor wax, fold my hands neatly on my lap, and consider staying in the janitor's closet for the rest of the day. But no. Mr. Mostella probably wouldn't welcome company. A silent, morose man, plagued by chewing gum, clogged toilets, starbursts of chocolate milk and catsup on the cafeteria walls, he has his own griefs.

There is this about guilt. It makes you behave. I float through the remainder of the day in an insulating bubble of sorrow, trying to do everything right. I extract a new and final deadline from Mr. Carruthers for the revision of my paper on *Catcher in the Rye*. Lucile avoids me. I avoid Dermot, who for some reason hovers in the middle distance every now and then with a pleading look in his eye. I even make an attempt to attend swimming, willing for once to stalk around the bottom of the pool like the Creature from the Black Lagoon while the legs of my classmates flutter overhead, angel limbs protruding from the clouds . . . I am shooed away by Miss Summers. I should see Mrs. Cuddleson about my case, she tells me. My case. It has come to this. I have acquired a case.

When I finally get home, the loft seems very empty. Abandoned. As if Catherine had carried off the household gods in her overnight bag. Cupboard doors swing open. A newspaper is scattered on the floor; a draft from a window left ajar frays the tattered curtains.

I wonder if she will come back. No, I don't really wonder about that. Mrs. Merkie will no doubt leave her on the doorstep Sunday night. What I wonder is if I want to be here to trade stories about our weekend. The guarded voices, the speculative glances. Is this to be endured? I look around for the answer to this question, but all I see is dust gathering in the corners of the room. Yes, nothing but dust and decay is all I see. And Celine-Beast peeking out of her newsprint pad. I give her a kick on my way to the bathroom.

I rummage through the medicine chest for some of Catherine's old makeup. Small cakes of powder. Mascara. The selection of lipstick is enormous. Some promises to taste of bubble gum. I can yet be cute. Cute enough to eat. While I dab and smear, I think about Celine-Beast. She didn't look so bad, really. It was just a quick look, but she seemed to have pulled herself together during the night. Drawings and paintings have a way of making adjustments for good or bad when you're not looking. I begin to feel hopeful as I examine myself in the mirror. The results are not cute, exactly. I don't seem to have Lucile's touch. But they are interesting.

I march out of the bedroom and confront Celine-Beast directly. Yes . . . Yes, yes, yes. There is something here, after all. The problem isn't with the shoulders. It's getting the weight and balance right. I whip out my charcoal and start working, and after a few minutes I'm pretty excited. This might just work, after all. Paint is the real test, of course. Paint is where it's at. (157)

I haul out the canvas that I was going to use on Lucile, fetch the long mirror from the bathroom door, prop it up on a chair, and strip off my pants and T-shirt and take a look.

Where is Celine-Beast? She is there somewhere. Broad hips and shoulders. That's Celine-Beast. And she's careless about shaving her legs and under her arms. No self-respect, my gramma would say, but Celine-Beast doesn't care. She likes stubble, and oh, that big blurry mouth. That's Celine-Beast without her mask. I blow out my stomach and bend my knees slightly, and Celine-Beast mugs right back at me. She's there, all right.

I start working fast then, blocking in shapes with yellow ocher and turpentine. Celine-Beast is big and fat, but the structure is all there. I can see it.

I don't know how long I've been working when the doorbell rings. Celine-Beast flees—she's shy—and there is poor skinny naked Celine staring out of the mirror. Caught being weird again.

"Catherine? Are you there?" It is Mrs. Barker.

"Yes. Just a minute." I can't find any of my clothes. Some fetishist has snuck in while I was working and carried off my entire wardrobe. Finally I discover one of Catherine's old bathrobes in the bathroom and open the door.

"Oh, Celine. Where's Catherine? Could you look after Jacob for a few minutes? I have to catch a plane at 7:30 and his father isn't here yet to pick him up. He must be on his way, because I just called and he wasn't there." Mrs. Barker stops to take in my bathrobe, which I am trying to tie up. "Did I awaken you?" she asks, all big eyes and wondering.

"No. That's okay. I was just going to take a bath and shave my legs." Mrs. Barker stares and I turn red, and then to my relief she decides to pretend I didn't say that.

"Well . . . if you don't really mind. I would appreciate it. It would just be for a few minutes, and I don't want to leave him alone." Her eyes fill with tears. I think we are both astonished.

"No, that's okay. He can stay here."

"I'm sorry." She takes out a tissue and blots under each eye, where her eyeliner threatens to run. Jake wanders in, all unconcerned. He must be getting used to his mother crying.

"It's just that he's so inconsiderate." She means Jake's father. "I thought if we were . . . if we weren't living together, I wouldn't have to put up with all his . . . all his . . ."

"Bad habits," I suggest, and she nods gratefully. "He's not just thoughtless, you know. I used to think that, but it isn't so. It's deliberate. He's so . . . so . . ."

"Manipulative."

"Yes. That's it. Manipulative. And now it's just the same. I still have to depend on him, and he's even more undependable. It's ridiculous, isn't it?"

"Well. It's just until Jake grows up."

She glances at Jake, who is studying my painting of Celine-Beast. She nods, but there is something disgruntled about the corners of her mouth. I realize that I am talking years here. Nobody wants to talk years when they're unhappy.

She sighs. "I really have to run now. Remind Jacob's father that I won't be back until Monday morning. He has an appointment tomorrow afternoon with Dr. Korbel." She fumbles in her purse. "Here's the appointment card. You'd better give him that. And tell him to get Jacob there on time. She was very annoyed last week."

I take the card. A little blue ticket. "Okay. I'll give it to him. Should you leave a note on your door?"

"Oh. Yes, of course. I think I already did." She blushes slightly and goes off down the stairs with her small suitcase and leather bag. Goodbye. Goodbye. Have a safe trip. I close the door.

"Is that you?" Jake asks, pointing at Celine-Beast.

"Yes. That's me."

He puts his little nose up until it's almost in the paint. "You're not really like that."

"Like what?"

"I don't know. Fat and crazy."

"Sometimes I am. Sometimes I'm just like that. Fat and crazy."

"No, you're not!" He grabs my hand and drags me

toward the couch, determined to save me from Celine-Beast. "Let's watch TV."

"You watch. I have to get dressed before your father gets here." My clothes seem to have magically reappeared. My jeans are in Catherine's bed and my shoes and socks are on a chair in the kitchen. I discover that I have been using my T-shirt as a paint rag.

"Do you want these?" Jake asks from the couch, holding up my underpants.

"Yes, thank you." I snatch them out of his prehensile fingers.

"You're welcome."

I shall never have any dignity again in my entire life.

In the bathroom I decide that maybe I really will take a bath. There is no need to be completely grubby when Mr. Barker gets here. A girl who isn't clean has no self-respect, is what my gramma always says. But what if I'm still in the tub? I mean, I have all these instructions I have to give him. Maybe I could wrap up in some snowy-white towel . . .

Jake pounds on the door. "Hey! Have you got anything to eat?"

I come out of my trance and close my mouth. "Yes. Just a minute." I will take a bath another day. Everything will be another day.

I need not have worried. Jake's father never shows. Jake and I spend an hour on the couch, watching television and eating peanut butter and jam on saltines. We are feeling sticky and sick of one another, and Jake yawns

and puts his feet up on the couch and starts kicking me
to relieve the monotony.

"Don't do that," I say. "You're getting my jeans dirty."

"They are already dirty."

My pants are dirty and the dust Jake is kicking out of
the couch cushions is drifting through the air. The washes
that I have used on Celine-Beast have turned to chalk
and the only thing I want to brush is my teeth.

"Cut it out, Jake. I'm going to call your father. Do
you know his number?"

He rattles it off.

"What? Slower. I can't remember it when you say it
that fast." Of course he can't remember it *unless* he says
it that fast, but finally we put something together with
the right number of digits. When I dial, there is no
answer. I let the phone ring twenty times.

"Are you sure this is the right number?"

"What number?"

I repeat it.

"Yeah. That's right." He is sitting up very straight, very
absorbed in the television. So absorbed that I realize
suddenly that he is pretending. Every now and then, he
gives me a look out of the corner of his eye. A distinctly
furtive look. He has something to hide.

My suspicions must show, because all at once he gives
a jump, just as if someone had stuck him in the behind.

"Oh!" he says. "I just remembered. He isn't there. He
had to do something else today."

"*What?*"

"He had to do something today. I forget what it was. He said I couldn't come over to his house." He makes his fingers do a dance on the arm of the couch to amuse me.

"What are you *talking* about, Jake? When did he tell you this?"

He has to think. Yesterday. Yes. That's right. It was definitely yesterday.

"Jacob. I don't get this. Does your mother know?"

No, he doesn't think so.

"Well, who did he talk to? Did he talk to you? Why didn't you tell your mother?"

He looks up from his fingers and tries to gauge what sort of story I might believe. "I forgot?" he asks. I shake my head. That's not the right answer.

"Well . . ." he says, very cutting because I am forcing him to say the obvious. "She would just get mad!"

"Well!" I say, marching around the room with my hands on my hips. "Well, I declare! And just where do you plan to stay this weekend, young man?" I sound exactly like my grandmother. Those would be her very words. Is this really the way I want to be? I mean, I do know why he didn't tell his mother. Being the peace-keeper in a family can be pretty heavy business. I remember once when my mother and father weren't talking to one another and I had to carry messages back and forth. My mother finally got so mad that she wouldn't give me any messages and I had to make them up . . . Oh, the strain of it all. I declare.

"Why can't I just stay here?" says Jake, round head swiveling like an owl's as he watches me gallop around.

"The reason is, I've got all this stuff to do, that's all."

"What stuff?" (163)

"I've got to write this paper about Holden Caulfield, for one thing."

"Who's he?"

"A fictitious person. A completely fictitious person."

"What's that?"

"Never mind." I flop down on the couch and stare at the television. A picture of a cooling tower at a nuclear plant. Huge, like an hourglass . . .

There is, I'm sure, something perfectly obvious that one does in circumstances like this, but all I can think of is to order a pizza. That can't be right. I should call the police, I suppose, so that they can scour the streets for Mr. Barker. Alert the Air National Guard and the president of Mrs. Barker's bank, so that she might be ferried home in record time . . . I sigh, deeply, from the heart. Jake, who knows complete capitulation when he sees it, snuggles up.

"Have you got anything else to eat?" he asks.

"Pizza. I'm going to order a pizza. Do you like pepperoni?"

"Let's order Chinese take-out," Jake says primly. "It's better for you." He pats me on the head. I might have expected this. I agree to let him stay the night and already he's taking over.

*   *   *

After we finish eating, Jake helps me carry the dirty dishes into the kitchen and watches me rinse them off before I stack them in the sink.

"Aren't you going to wash them?"

"No. There aren't enough yet."

"You're supposed to wash them right away. My mom always does. So you won't get bugs."

"We already have bugs. Mel Hollingsford's bugs. He asked us to take care of them while he was gone."

"No, he didn't."

"If you're so worried about bugs, you wash them. I'm going to take a bath."

"Why do I have to? You're the grownup."

I drape a dish towel over his head so I won't have to see him anymore and go in the bathroom and lock the door. I think I will begin a new life. A quite different life. Take charge, as they say. I can be anything I want. Anything at all. And what will that be, I ask myself, getting in the tub. I shall first of all be a person who never finishes the revision of her American literature theme. A terrific sense of well-being fills my soul.

Jake pounds on the door. Wow. Perhaps I'll be a child murderer.

"What do you want, Jake? I'm taking a bath."

"I have to go."

"Hold it. I'm in the bathtub already."

"No. I really, really have to go now!" I can hear him doing a tap dance outside.

This is a plot, I suspect, but it would be a real crisis

if he went in his pants. It's not something I want to deal with.

I nearly break my neck trying to reach the lock from the tub, and collapse with a splash as he comes charging in, struggling with his zipper. He really does have to go, but he wants to look, too, and the combination is bad for his aim.

"Pee first. Look later, Jake."

He guffaws like a miniature dirty old man and admires the ceiling. When he is finished, he fastens his pants and comes over with all due solemnity for a look. I subside in the soapsuds and feel grumpy.

"You've got hair," he observes.

"Yes. It's normal."

"Yeah. My mom's got hair."

"No doubt. She also is a grownup."

"You've got more than my mom." This is the most tedious conversation I have ever had in my life. I mean that truly. It even surpasses discussions of belly-button lint or those news reports on the state of the President's intestines.

"Maybe she's still going to grow up some more. Now get out of here, Jake. Right now." I grab Catherine's razor out of the soap dish to show him that our little discussion is at an end.

"What are you going to do with that?"

I am never going to forgive Jacob's parents for doing this to me. Why do I have to suffer just because their marriage is coming apart?

"I am going, Jacob—since you ask—I'm going to cut it all off. All my hair."

He retreats to the door, definitely alarmed. "You better not!"

"Yes, I am. I'm going to be a little kid. Just like you. I have decided that I am not going to be a grownup and that you're going to have to do the dishes from now on."

"I'll tell your mom!"

"So? My mom is at present living her second childhood on a yacht in the Bahamas. She will be very pleased," I say, and grab for the can of shaving cream.

"She will not! You're going to have to go to jail!" Jake yells and scuttles off. So he won't be an accessory, I suppose.

I finish my bath in peace. I find a new white sweat suit that Catherine has washed and hidden behind the towels. It is men's extra-large and just my size. I will not have to go to jail. I'm very confident about that. A mental institution, maybe, but not jail.

I wash the dishes. I sweep the floor. I take out the garbage. Every now and then, Jacob's little head bobs up over the back of the couch to see what I am doing. When I smile sweetly at him, he frowns and ducks down again.

When the phone rings, I answer it. I'm in complete control of my life.

"Celine? We've got to talk."

"Who is this, please."

"Dermot. I'm over at McDonald's and I . . ."

"Dermot who?" I say, praying that this is a knock-knock joke.

"Dermot! What's the matter with you?"

"Oh. Hi, Dermot. Just a second. Jake? Don't do that." Jake has poured himself a glass of milk and is trying to stand the carton up on a couch cushion beside him. (167)

"Hey!" Dermot yells in my ear. "Is *he* there?"

"Who?"

"*Him!* The guy you went to the country with."

Oh, yeah. *Him!*

"Listen, Dermot. Nobody's here. I don't want to talk to you. I don't want to see you. I am going . . ."

"You can tell him I'm going to push his face in. No. I'll tell him. Put him on the phone. Let me talk to this . . . this Jake the Snake."

"Screw you, Dermot. I want you to leave me alone. Jake is a weight lifter, too, and he's even hunkier than you are, and if you don't . . ."

"Oh, yeah? How much can he press?"

"What?" This is a mysterious question he is asking.

"Come on. What can he press? I can press over three hundred."

"So? *I* can press the Sears Tower if I'm standing next to it." I have a vision of myself, pressed up tight against the dark tower. It's kind of exciting, in a way.

"What?" Now Dermot is confused. This isn't a conversation. I am talking with a space probe from the planet Vulcan. I detach the phone from my ear, where it is trying to take root, and hang up. Then I pick it up again and let it dangle. I'm busy. From now on, as far as Dermot is concerned, I am busy.

"Come on, Jake," I say. "Time to get ready for bed."

"Who was that?

"It was a wrong number. You're going to sleep on the couch, all right?"

"Yeah. If it was a wrong number, why were you talking to him on the telephone?"

"He had to be persuaded."

Jake helps me spread some sheets and a blanket. We plump up a pillow together. He keeps giving me stern, dubious looks.

"What's the matter with you?" I ask.

His eyes narrow and his lower lip pops out like a cash-register drawer. "Did you?" he says.

"Did I what?"

"You know!" He snarls, milk teeth all ready to bite.

"Oh, that. No, I didn't, but it's none of your business anyway."

Jake turns disdainful and looks down his nose. "You'd have to go to jail," he says. He's telling me, I am to understand, for my own good.

"No, I wouldn't, you goof."

"Yes, you would. It's against the law." He's taken off his jeans and flannel shirt now, and I can see why he speaks with such authority. He's wearing Superman underwear. It's amazing. I have been entertaining Clark Kent and didn't even know it.

"Can I ask you something?" I say. "There's something I've always wanted to know. What happens to the clothes you leave in the phone booth? Do you go back and get them later, or just write them off as a business expense?"

Jacob gives me a funny look, but I never do learn his secret, because at that moment the doorbell rings.

"Hey," I say, with more hope than reason. "That must be your dad." I am relieved, of course, but not so relieved, because I realize suddenly that unless I can think of some way to keep Mr. Barker here I'm going to be left all alone, and not even the dirty dishes to occupy me. As I open the door, I am ready to offer coffee, leftover egg rolls, a life of pure devotion.

In bounces Dermot. "Okay," he says, "where is he?" He sniffs the air and paws the ground. His keen eye scans the room, but apparently the only way to draw his attention to Jacob is to make an introduction.

"You mean Jake the Snake," I say. "Jake the Snake? Meet Dermot the Demented."

"Dermot the who?" says Jake. He and Dermot study each other warily for a moment, and then Dermot nods at me with this wry sneer. "Very cute. Real cute. You're real cute, Celine."

"Yes. I know. Totally cute. Well. Now you've met him. So." I hint with my eyes that the door is still open.

"Okay, I'm going, I'm going," he says. "It was that business with Beth the other night, wasn't it? That's what bothers you, isn't it?"

"No, Dermot. That didn't bother me at all."

"Yeah, I thought that was it. Listen, Celine. I just wanted to tell you I feel really bad about that. I could hardly sleep last night." He shakes his head in sad amazement. "I kept wondering what you must think about me."

"The truth is, Dermot, I never give you a moment's thought."

"Yeah. I mean, you must think I'm some sort of animal or something. But I'm not really. It's just that . . . Well, men are different from women. We have these physical drives, you know, and you can't just bottle them up all of the time. It just isn't possible."

"Well, that certainly is interesting, Dermot. But I . . ."

"I'm not saying it's your fault. I mean, I know you've led this real sheltered life, and you don't want to rush into things. I respect that." He turns bug-eyed out of respect. "I really do." He allows me a small rueful smile. "You want to know something really strange? I wouldn't want you any different. I like you just the way you are."

"Great, Dermot. That's very reassuring, but . . ."

"Yeah. I knew you'd understand. Well, I'm sorry. What else can I say?" He smiles at me helplessly and holds out his arms. I think I am supposed to leap into them.

"How about goodbye?"

"What?" I seem finally to have his attention.

"How about bottling up your physical drives long enough to find the door."

There is a pause while Dermot works out the implications of this remark for our relationship. As he does so, he begins to turn red, and his neck begins to swell above his collar.

"That is so witty, Celine. You are so witty."

"Yes. Totally witty. Now get out of here."

"I should have listened to Tiffany, you know that? She saw right through you. The great artist. Going around and sneering at . . . at important things. Making fun all the time of . . . of family values. You know what? I can't figure out why I ever liked you at all."

"It is certainly a puzzle, Dermot. Why don't you and Tiffany talk it over?"

"All right, all right," he says. "I'm going." But he doesn't. He wanders over to Celine-Beast and sneers at her for a while.

"The great artist . . . Who's this supposed to be?" He takes in the mirror propped up against the chair. "It's supposed to be you, isn't it. What have you been doing, anyway? Standing around naked and painting yourself? Talk about creeps."

"Get out, Dermot. Right now."

"Yeah, yeah . . ." He looks at Jake, who is standing there in his Superman underwear. Dermot frowns. "What's going on here, anyway? Where's your step-mother? Why doesn't he have his clothes on?"

"Go! Just please go!" I say, and catch his arm and try to pull him toward the door. What do I think I am doing? He doesn't resist, but he doesn't move, either. It's like pulling on the Statue of Liberty. Worse yet, I tear the shoulder of this flimsy jacket he is wearing. Not a bad tear. The sleeve just separates a little.

"Hey!" he yells. "Watch the jacket. You know how much this cost? A hundred and fifty bucks." He takes off the jacket and examines it, as if it were a family heirloom. He is frowning and very red in the face, but I can see that underneath he's really pleased I've torn his stupid jacket.

"Come on, Dermot. I'll send you a check."

"Just a minute. Just a damned minute." Oh, he is really happy now. "How would you like it if people went around tearing your clothes?" I see this big hand slowly, almost reluctantly, reaching out for my sweatshirt, and I wonder what is going to happen.

Jake gives Dermot a sudden hard shove. "You leave her alone! You're not supposed to be here! You go home!"

Dermot looks around in confusion and finally locates Jacob. "Hey," he says. "No violence."

"You! You no violence! You're not the boss of me, you know!" Jacob can be very sarcastic when he wants.

"Yes!" I shout. "You get out of here, Dermot. You get out right now." I fetch the baseball bat that Catherine keeps in the wastebasket by the door in case of burglars. "You're just a bully, Dermot. You think you're so great, but you're just a big bully."

Dermot licks his lips and his eyes dart around. He is not afraid of my baseball bat, but he is confused. He thought he was playing the heavy in a daytime soap, but the script is turning into Looney Tunes.

"You know what's the matter with you, Celine?" he says, falling back on that subject of endless fascination. "You never grew up. You should try it."

"You! You grow up. You're just a big fat baby. You don't know anything."

"Yeah," Jake chimes in. "You fib. You fib all the time."

"You're crazy," Dermot mutters, trying to make a dignified exit, but it is Jake who gets in the last word. I almost slam his fat little head in the door, he's so anxious to deliver the last crushing blow. "Liar! Liar! Pants . . ."

I pull Jake back, lock the door, and my knees decide they've been holding me up long enough for one day.

"Pants on fire!" Jake yells out the window. He leans far out, watching, he must be, until Dermot has disappeared, and then he swaggers over to where I'm sitting on the floor, flexing his powerful muscles.

"Boy, he was really dumb," he says. My Superhero.

ELEVEN/

The next morning Jacob and I are eating French toast and watching this program about the problem of being married to an unbeliever when, of all people, who should call but Catherine.

"I just wanted to be sure you were okay," she says.

"Yes, I'm okay. Are you okay?" I ask, a little alarmed. My first thought is that she has been hit by a car and is on her deathbed and wants to get everything straight between us before she passes away.

"Yes, I'm okay," she says sharply. "Why shouldn't I be okay? Is something wrong?"

"With you? I don't know. Is something wrong with you?"

"With me? Should there be something wrong with me? Am I okay?" she says, a note of hysteria creeping into her voice.

"No, no. You're okay." There is a long pause.

"You're sure?" she says. About what, I wonder, but don't ask.

"Yes, but listen, Catherine. The weirdest thing happened . . ." I say, and tell her all about how Jacob got left with me and his father never came to pick him up. While I'm chatting away I begin to realize that my role in this drama has definite possibilities. I mean, here is this helpless child left on my hands in the middle of the night. Decisions have to be made quickly. Pizza or Chinese takeout? Well, that doesn't sound too impressive, but I'm sure with some editing . . . I have visions of a small item in the *Tribune*: LOCAL GIRL SHOWS A LITTLE MATURITY ". . . and so I'm going to take him over to his father's studio this morning and see if he's there. Mr. Barker, I mean. What do you think? Pretty responsible, right?"

"Hmm? Yes, that's very nice. Listen, Celine. I called your father last night."

"Really? In Paris?"

"No. He's in Frankfurt."

"Oh. I thought he was in Paris. Why do you suppose . . ."

"Just shut up a minute, Celine, and listen." There is an appropriate pause while I demonstrate that I have shut up. Catherine takes a deep breath. "We had a long talk about a lot of things, and he's coming back as soon as he can. He thinks he can get a flight Monday."

"Oh."

"You don't sound exactly thrilled."

"No, I am thrilled, really." Actually, I'm stunned. This jaunt to Madison with Professor Merkie and his mother must have been a real blowout. Catherine sounds almost human. I have a sudden vision of her sitting alone on a bed in a motel room at two o'clock in the morning, staring first at the industrial-strength carpet and then at the telephone . . . It's very moving, really.

"Well . . . anyway, we talked things over and we decided that it might be a good idea if we took a long vacation together. The three of us, after school is out."

"Oh. Great."

"I thought we might go camping or something like that. We have to do something. We've all been under a lot of strain, and I think we have to spend some time together and do some serious talking."

"Yeah. Sure."

"You don't sound sure."

"I would like that. I mean, going camping together."

"Well. We'll talk about it some more when I get home. We seem to have difficulty communicating over the phone."

"Yeah, we do, don't we? Are you sure you're okay? I mean, is it a good conference and all?"

"It's a bloody bore," says Catherine. "The whole thing is bloody, bloody awful. I may come home early. Catch a bus or something."

I make the appropriate sympathetic noises. We say

goodbye cheerfully. Why, as I turn back to the television, do I feel so treacherous? So divided? I think I understand how Catherine feels. This is a real olive branch she's offering, isn't it? It should make me happy, but it doesn't. I don't want to go camping with her and my father. That's the truth. The thought of us all working out our problems simply fills me with exhaustion. This must be unnatural, I think, my eyes focusing on a faith healer on TV going down a row of little old ladies. He twists up their canes and bops them on the head with the palm of his hand. They fall backwards into waiting arms. Will they be caught? This is the real test of their faith, I suspect. They steel themselves; their weak arms flutter . . . I picture Catherine, my father, and me gathered around the camp-fire in our three-piece suits. Why don't I have any faith? Maybe I am an unbeliever. Or maybe it's simply too late.

"Who was that?" Jacob asks.

"What? Oh, that was just Catherine. She wanted to see if we were okay."

"Oh. She's not your real mother, is she?"

"Catherine? No, of course not. She's just somebody my father married. After he and my mom split."

"Why don't you live with your mom, then? Is she dead?"

"No, she's not dead. She's living in South America. In Brazil. Go get your coat. We've got to go find your father."

Jake gets up wearily and fetches his jacket. "Well, why don't you live with her, then?"

"With my mother? Ah, well . . . She has this very important job, you see. Taking care of this old guy who's trying to cut down the rain forests before he dies. It's a very responsible job. It takes all her energy. The National Security Agency is very interested."

"That's not true," Jacob says, twisting and pulling as I try to zip up his coat. "That's not even funny."

"No. No, you're right. That's not even very funny. I don't know. I must be slipping." I turn off the television and drag him out the door.

"Nobody ever tells me anything," he grumbles. He is unstrung by the injustice of it all and shambles down the hall, his head wagging with grief. "Nobody ever ever tells me anything . . ."

Shortly before noon, Jake and I are heading west on Superior Street in the new gallery district. We peer through windows at enormous canvases heavy with paint and texture or, in one place, tiny irregularities of wood and wire, each clinging to the center of a wall like a bug. Jake is very critical.

"Look at those," he says. "I could do that, but I wouldn't." I have to stop and explain then. How it may seem that he could do those, but he couldn't really. That they have qualities that are not apparent to the uninitiated.

"What qualities?"

"Well, it's a matter of context. I mean, to you it just looks like the end of an orange crate hanging on a wall with a screwdriver sticking in it, but . . ."

"That's what it is."

"What?"

"The end of an orange crate hanging on the wall with a screwdriver sticking in it."

"So? The *Mona Lisa* is just a piece of rag with some paint on it. Come on. We're going to be late."

He lets me drag him away, a smug look on his face because he knows the end of an orange crate when he sees one and doesn't appreciate the transforming magic of context.

And of course it is difficult to explain why such a thing should deserve our attention. Ordinarily, we wouldn't look at all. And yet we do when it's hanging there on a wall in artful light.

Perhaps it's the money. This is a work of art because it costs so much. We see things there because they are washed with a wonderful glaze of gold. It's a sobering thought, really. To understand that those busy men and women working away in law offices and in the commodity markets are the ultimate artists, creating works of art without even looking, simply because they are willing to pay so much.

It's hard to keep Jake moving. He grows more reluctant as we get closer to the address written down on my piece of paper towel. He stops to admire some newly installed antique streetlights, sits down on the curb to retie his shoes.

"He's probably not there," he says.

"What do you mean? He said he'd be there. Painting his studio institutional green."

"He's probably working. He doesn't like it when people hang around when he's working."

"So? He'll need a break. He'll welcome us with open arms."

But of course, when we do locate the studio on the top floor of an old building and lean on the bell, nothing happens. Jake goes off to investigate a young woman in black leather who is painting a large poster on the floor at the end of the hall, while I stare at the door a little longer. It is made of metal, with a tiny peephole like a navel. I peer through it and see nothing at all. Mrs. Barker is right, I suppose. Her husband is very, very unreliable.

Jake comes back and grabs my hand. "Let's go," he says. "She told me to bugger off."

I glare at the leather girl, who is picking her nose and staring at us with revolutionary distaste.

"Let's go beat her up, then. Let's go beat her up and then take her to lunch at the Under-the-El Deli."

Jake doesn't answer, because he is watching a couple coming toward us down the hall. They are wearing old clothes stained with off-white paint and carrying paper bags of take-out food. They are also necking, difficult as that may be, loaded as they are with food and walking and Mr. Barker's divorce not even final so far as I know. Miss Denver holds up her chin so he can bend and kiss her on the throat. When she catches sight of me, she detaches herself from Mr. Barker with the neat violence of a pilot ejecting from a starfighter. She blushes. A trifle embarrassed. That is her reaction. My own impulse is to fall over flat on my back or, more in character perhaps, walk around in tiny circles, clutching my stomach and whimpering. I am more heartbroken than I would have thought possible. I hadn't wanted so very much from Mr. Barker. To paint the walls together. Make soup on a hot (181) plate, share a glass of wine in a cracked cup, watch Jake run around a big empty room roaring like a jet. Talk.

"Celine!" Miss Denver cries. "What are you doing here? Hitting the galleries?" She comes toward Jake and me, still flustered at having been caught with a sex life by a student, but not really caring, because she is so happy about her life. She is radiant. Her cheeks glow, her pale eyes glisten with tears. "Did you see Kraut's new things at Marianne Deson? They're terrific. Really terrific. This is Paul Barker. The painter. He's a real hotshot, so you should get to know him. Come here, and don't make such a face, Paul. You're not that modest. Anyway, this is Celine Morienval. She's a painter, too. Really good."

Mr. Barker stalks up like a mechanical man. He is so shaken at the sight of us that I can hear him rattle. Abruptly his hand comes up, like that of a puppet whose string has been pulled. I'm not sure at first what I'm supposed to do with it, but then I give it a little shake.

"Hi," he says.

"Did you make up your mind about *Test Patterns* yet?" Miss Denver asks. "It's this painting that Celine did, Paul." She can't resist putting her arm around his waist and giving him a big possessive hug. "It's really . . . I'm trying to get her to submit it to the Institute show." She smiles at me, rubbing her cheek against Mr. Barker's shoulder.

"I can't," I admit finally. At long last. "I ruined it. It's completely ruined. That's why I can't submit it."

For a moment Miss Denver doesn't know what to say. Her smile fades; she bites her lower lip. "Well. I'm sure there'll be others. Don't get hung up about it. There'll be others." To change the subject, she squats down so that her face is at Jacob's level. His feet are firmly planted, but he twists his head to frown at the girl in leather on her knees at the end of the hall.

"Who's this?" says Miss Denver. "What's your name?"

"Jake."

"Oh. Hi, Jake. I'm Angie." She tries to catch his hands in hers. "Are you Celine's little brother? Listen. Don't be shy. I'm her art teacher. At school. Did she tell you that at the end of the year we have an open house? Everybody can come and see all the things the art students have made this year. Would you like to do that? Are you a painter, too?"

Jacob's head swivels to face her. "No," he says, so coolly that Miss Denver's eyes cloud. He very deliberately pushes her hands away and then takes mine. "Come on. Let's go."

They fit exactly, his hand and mine. It seems a long time ago that Miss Denver and I bent our heads together over Miss Piggy pencil holders and spoke of the messiness of love. And still we didn't know.

"Okay," I whisper and pull him close, but I have to look at Mr. Barker one last time. I want to know if he is

going to let us walk away down the hall, just like that.
He must realize that would be impossible. And yet. And
yet he is such a very careless man.

"Wait a second," he says, coming back to life with a (183)
jerk. He takes a deep breath and squeezes his nose until
his eyes water. "Angie? This is Jacob. My son, Jacob. He
and his mother live in the same building. With Celine.
We've already, uh, met."

Miss Denver, still crouched beside Jacob, lifts her
face to Mr. Barker. The smile with which she wanted to
charm is now puzzled and frightened. "But why didn't
you . . . ?" she begins. She looks at her ink-stained hands
and then stands up slowly. Her knees crack, as if she has
just that moment grown old.

"I think I've been making a fool of myself," she says.

"No," says Mr. Barker. He touches her shoulder gin-
gerly. "I wanted you to meet. Just not this way."

"No. Not this way."

"Well. It can't be helped. Listen." He bounces on his
heels and looks wild. "Why don't we all have lunch.
We've got plenty of stuff . . ."

"We've got to go," says Jake. His shoulders are held
so rigidly they almost hum with tension. "We've got a
'pointment."

His father sighs. "Listen, Jacob. I know you're upset,
but . . ." Jacob turns and walks off down the hall toward
the stairs, and then Miss Denver walks away, too. She
steps carefully over the poster that the girl in black leather
is painting. She stares out the window there, holding her

shoulders as if she might suddenly fold herself up into something small and square.

Mr. Barker watches them both move away. First Jake and then Miss Denver. He sways slightly, but his feet seem nailed to the floor. He clears his throat and considers the packages he is holding.

"When you see Jean, tell her it's not a good idea to send Jacob over without letting me know he's coming. It's not a good idea at all." He looks at me sharply. "If she does it again, I'll break her neck."

Out in the street, Jacob won't talk to me. He is too absorbed in the feel of a brick wall, an oil slick on the pavement. As we walk toward the Ravenswood El, he dribbles a small stone in front of him with his feet, until I try to get into the act. When the pebble lands in front of me, I pass it back to him, and then he steps over it as if it weren't there. He keeps his distance.

Outside the Under-the-El Deli I ask him if he wants something to eat. He stops to think, to gauge how far he will be compromised by even admitting that he has heard me, and then shrugs his shoulders and follows me inside.

"What do you want?" I ask. "A ham sandwich?" Another shrug. He traces the reflection of the black girders of the El track in the glass front of the counter with his fingers. When we sit down at one of the small tables near the windows, he turns his chair so that he won't be obliged to look at me.

Three young ballet students are gathered around the cash register, bundling up thousands of calories in greasy paper. Two are wearing modesty wraps, but the third and most beautiful has nothing on but a shimmering bodysuit. The men in the deli can't take their eyes off her. Her hands flutter around the shoulders of her friends and the three of them make strange insect sounds together.

"Is that a good sandwich?" I ask. A dumb question. Maybe it deserves to be ignored completely. "Listen, Jake. I'm sorry about this, but let's not make a big deal out of it, okay? I mean finally, really finally I mean, it's not going to make much difference. You were going to have to meet her sometime anyway. And she's nice. Really nice. The next time . . ."

"I don't want to talk about it."

"No. No, I know you don't, but . . ."

"I said I don't want to talk about it!" Jacob looks at me now, furious. "You talk all the time."

I watch a train rattle by on the tracks overhead. It isn't fair. I hadn't meant it to be like this at all.

"What are you mad at me for? It's your dad who's the jerk."

"He is not a jerk!" Jacob says, squeezing the ham right out of his sandwich. "You're the jerk. The big fat jerk!"

"Listen. I didn't . . ."

"I told you we shouldn't go! I told you and I told you!" His face buckles with grief. "Now he's going to be so mad at me . . ."

"No, he's not, Jacob. Really he's not. It's not your fault."

He doesn't even hear me, rocking back and forth in his chair, holding up his sandwich with his little hands. "He's going to be so mad."

"It's not your fault, Jacob!"

His eyes spring open with revelation. "It's your fault! It's all your fault! You big dumb!"

"Well. Maybe I am a big dumb. I certainly don't know what I'm doing here. If you want to go back and stay with your dad, that's fine with me. I've got other things to do. I'm not going to be around here much longer, that's for sure. In two weeks I'm heading for Italy, and you know something? I can hardly wait. Maybe I should leave tomorrow. Why not? No problem . . ."

"Yes, you go! You're just a big dumb. Nobody likes you . . ." He looks around for the words to kill me with, he is so furious. "That's why you don't live with your mom. You do such dumb things she doesn't like you anymore. She doesn't want you anymore!"

Overhead, another train passes on the El tracks. There are no guardrails, nothing to hold the train down but gravity. Day after day, year after year, it does this. Through all the rain and snow. Through all the talk. It's hard not to believe that there won't be a moment when the last word is said and gravity will fail. When all the laws of the universe that hold things together fatigue and let go. The dancing girls will cram their mouths full even as the customers at the Under-the-El tear at their clothes and the train finally loses its grip on the rails and plunges through our window.

"Eat your sandwich, Jake. We're going to be late for Dr. Korbel."

TWELVE /

"There you are, Jacob," says a woman standing by the receptionist's desk. "We were beginning to wonder." She smiles at us over a handful of manila folders. She has soft brown hair tumbling down around her shoulders, and clear green eyes. Jake turns shy and tries to occupy the space I've already claimed, standing on my feet and knocking his head against my stomach.

"I'm sorry we're late," I begin. "There was some sort of mix-up this morning." As I try to explain, I nudge Jake steadily forward with my knees, my hands on his shoulders.

"I see," says the woman, watching us attentively. "I'm

Dr. Korbel," she adds when we are close enough to shake hands. "Are you a friend of the family?" The receptionist, a middle-aged woman whose hair is as fluffy and golden as that of a child, raises her eyes and studies me across her desk. She looks suspicious, but I don't hesitate, not wanting to think about the question, it seems so enormously complicated.

"Yes," I say. "My name is Celine. Celine Morienval."

"Well," says Dr. Korbel. "I'm sorry Mr. Barker wasn't able to come. I did want to speak to him. But we'll just have to manage. Why don't we go down to the playroom, Jacob? You can wait here, Celine." She shows me into a kind of waiting room filled with comfortable furniture, heavy green plants, and no windows. They should give more thought to windows when they plan these places, I think as she leaves me. I feel so solemn and edgy.

A woman in a pink pants suit has evidently been waiting for me. She edges forward slightly in her chair, her large purse clasped firmly on her plump knees. Am I waiting to see Dr. Metcalf, she asks.

"No. I'm just waiting for a friend."

She sighs deeply. "Yes. Aren't we all?"

I don't know what to say to this, not having meant to be so profound. A girl of about twelve is stretched out on a leather sofa, her long bare legs arranged to be admired. They are very pretty—pale, with a moist sheen as if they had been dipped in milk.

"We're waiting to see Dr. Metcalf. He's supposed to be very good with children," says the woman. "We were referred," she adds thoughtfully. The girl sits up abruptly, finds a cigarette in a small ragged bag of stonewashed denim.

"You don't mind if we smoke, I hope," says the (189) woman.

"No. That's okay."

"Thank you. Some people don't seem to appreciate how annoying it can be." The girl crosses her legs and flicks minute bits of ash on the carpet.

"That's a lovely sweater you have on," continues the woman. "I hope you don't mind my saying so. I'm in the design business, so I notice such things. It looks hand-knit. Did your mother make it for you?"

"No. It belongs to a friend, actually. I just borrowed it."

"Well, it's really lovely. It looks very nice on you. Not everything would, of course, given your particular coloring. I mean, that dead-white skin. So attractive. It's so important for a person to realize what is possible for them to wear. Simply because something looks nice on a model doesn't mean it will look nice on you. Some people never seem to realize that."

The girl stubs out her cigarette in a plant with fleshy leaves and sweeps a pile of old magazines onto the floor with a single wave of her hand. The woman allows herself a small, prim smile, but doesn't take her eyes off me.

"Oh," I say.

"Yes. Some people simply have no taste themselves. We have to admit that, don't we? It's not a fault, not to have any taste, but then you have to listen to those who do, don't you? What some people wear . . . Well, I have to laugh, being in the design business." She shows me then how she has to laugh. Amused, but there is a note of sadness. "Take your haircut, for example. You don't mind me talking about your hair, do you? I wouldn't say a word, but it's so becoming, cut short like that. Like a boy's haircut. Your hair is coarse—I don't mean that in a critical way. Coarse hair is really best—and your head is rather long . . . Some people would look ridiculous with a haircut like that, but on you it looks exactly right. Some people think just because the Princess of Wales looks great with a certain kind of haircut that they will, too. Your mother must have wonderful taste."

"Well . . ." I begin, but I'm distracted by the girl, who gets up suddenly and crosses the room to stand in front of me. She puts her hands on her boy hips and tilts her head to one side as she eyes me. "Are you in high school or what?" she asks.

"Come on, now," says the woman, who still wants to talk about my mother. "Give credit where credit is due, I always say. Does your mother help you with your shopping?"

"Yes. A junior." I say to the girl, and then to the woman: "Well, actually she's traveling in South America now."

"Oh, wow, a junior. Let me kiss your goddamn shoes before I pass out," says the girl.

"Oh, what a wonderful thing to do," says the woman. "There are other mothers who would love to travel in

South America if it weren't for the responsibilities which keep them practically tied in knots. Not that they mind, of course. But still, it is a sacrifice. We all have to admit that."

"Have you ever been to South America?" says the girl. "I know a guy from South America. Puerto Rico. He's really dreamy."

"Doesn't your mother worry about you? No, of course not. I can tell that you're a very responsible person. Some people . . . well, they simply have no self-respect. That's what it boils down to, doesn't it? I mean, some people . . . You turn your head for a moment and they run off with some alcoholic twice their age."

"He's got hair all over. He really likes me to bite the hair on his chest." The girl nudges my knees with hers.

"Of course, anyone who would do that has problems. We have to admit that, don't we? Too many hormones or something like that. What can you do? You have to help them, even if they think they don't need it."

"Have you got any money?" asks the girl suddenly. I glance at the woman, who just as suddenly begins to frown at a lamp across the room. Its stoneware base, its parchment shade absorb every fiber of her being.

"Well, a little," I say.

"Give me a dollar. I want to buy a Coke."

I fish some change out of my jeans and give it to her. Nothing else seems possible.

"Thanks, buggerbrain." The girl gives me a quick happy smile and disappears.

"Well!" says the woman. "Just imagine. Asking complete strangers for money. Some people think the world owes them a living, like her father, and the amazing thing is, how many people encourage them. I don't mean you, of course. A young girl like you is simply too inexperienced to know what is . . ."

(192)

A man in a bow tie and a tweed jacket so hairy that it looks as if it must have leapt upon him from ambush sticks his head in the door.

"Mrs. Barchluss?" he says cheerfully. The woman favors him with a modest smile, and the man lets himself in, all bouncy and energetic. "I'm Dr. Metcalf. Sorry to keep you waiting so long. We're running a little late, and of course I wanted to look over . . . over . . . over her file before . . . If you don't mind, I'll just have a little chat with . . . with this young lady . . ." He holds out his hand to me, and I accept it gratefully. ". . . and then perhaps you and I can . . . can . . . can decide what . . . what . . . what to do next." As he talks to Mrs. Barchluss over his shoulder, he shepherds me through the door, and I am safe at last.

"That was incredible," I exclaim, quite beside myself with relief. He ducks his head and steers me down the hall and into an office with a desk and a sink. "I mean, she was right there. If I wasn't supposed to give her any money, why didn't she say so? It was truly incredible. I feel almost as if I hallucinated the whole thing."

"Yes, yes, yes," says Dr. Metcalf like a cheerful little machine gun. He seems like a very understanding person.

"And the worst thing was that weird smile. Did you

notice it? As if her lips had been sewn shut and she *liked* it."

Dr. Metcalf motions me into a chair, and as I sit down I try to do an imitation of the woman's smile. It is something of a shock to see that he is smiling at me in exactly the same way.

"She really upsets you, doesn't she?" he says. Why do I have the feeling that "yes" is the wrong answer? That behind the mirror over the washbasin is someone in a dark room watching?

"Well," I say, going all shifty. "Sort of."

"That's interesting. Why do you think that is"—he moves his forearm slightly and glances at a pad of paper on his desk—"Sunshine?"

Isn't he a flirt, I think, but still I'm troubled, because no one has ever called me Sunshine before. Dr. Metcalf must sense my confusion, because he says almost at once, "You don't like to be called Sunshine, do you? What would you like me to call you?"

I hesitate, and then we exchange sly, conspiratorial smiles.

"Celine."

"Celine. That's a nice name. A *French* name," he informs me. He makes a note on his pad. "Well, Celine. Why don't you tell me why she upsets you so much?"

This is the first time I've ever been in a psychologist's office, and I really do appreciate the experience, but I realize I'm here under false pretenses, and so I try to straighten everything out without any further waffling around.

"Listen, Dr. Metcalf," I explain. "I think you've got me mixed up. I'm not supposed to be here."

"You're not?" He's even more interested than before.

"No. The person you're supposed to be talking to is the other one. The one who called me buggerbrain."

"She called you buggerbrain? That wasn't very nice."

"No. It wasn't." For some unaccountable reason, I feel my eyes fill with tears. "It wasn't very nice at all. But anyway she's the one you're supposed to be counseling. I don't have any problems like that. Like hers, I mean. Well, I don't know what her problems are exactly, but she seemed kind of screwed up."

"And you're fine. No problems."

"Well. I suppose everyone's got *some* problems."

"That's true, Celine. Very true. Now why don't we forget about her problems. Just tell me what's troubling *you*."

We peer deep into one another's eyes, and I feel as if I'm poised on the crest of a great ocean wave. It's traveled halfway around the globe, and now it's ready to break. How can it be resisted?

"Well . . ." I say, glancing away and back again so that he will have every opportunity to stop me. "*Well* . . . When I said I shouldn't be here . . . I mean I'm not even supposed to be in *Chicago*. My mom wants me to live with her, or anyway I *think* she wants me to live with her, but the guy she's been living with in Antigua

. . . well, he's kind of strange . . ." I look up at Dr. Metcalf to see how this is going down, and I detect a shadow of perplexity in his candid eyes. He glances down at his pad of paper, but there's no holding back now. I can feel the wave surge beneath me irresistibly. "He's really old and he keeps getting me mixed up with his sister who died in the influenza epidemic in 1918, and so every time he sees me he starts yelling, 'Florence? Is that you, Florence?' and nearly has a heart attack, and so of course I couldn't go there, and so my father had to take me because my grandmother said, 'No more, not after Oozing Baby.'—that's a rock band I was managing in Iowa—and that was okay because I like my dad and all, but he's married this little jerk who's only six years older than I am, and I know for a fact that she comes from Paterson, New Jersey, even though she has this phony English accent and keeps talking about Derrida all the time. I mean, I thought it was a musical comedy or something. I can even hear the music in my head. You know . . . *Derr-i-da, da-da-da, tum, tiddy-tum, tiddy-tum, tiddy-tum* . . . But that was okay, too, because as soon as school's out I was going to move to Florence and live with my friend Sybil, who's not a monster just because she thinks my dad is a sexist pig, and all I had to do was show a little maturity. But then my dad runs away on this long lecture tour and Catherine gets mixed up with this assistant professor down at Circle campus who is really right out of the waxworks and he keeps talking about how art is impossible in these decadent times and the only thing an artist can do is parody the aspirations of the past, until I am really ready to scream. And then I had this sort of thing for this guy who's old enough to be my father . . . He's Jake's father, actually—he's the reason I'm here, by the way—and I know that that would really be a dumb thing to get involved in, but he was nice to me, and you must know since you're a doctor that sometimes you do things even when you know it is positively stupid, like when I pushed that navy bean up my nose . . . but I'll tell you about that later, I mean if you think it's important that we go deep into my child-hood experience. But about this guy, I must have been out of my head, because the person he really likes is my art teacher, Miss Denver, and she's nice and the right age, so why do I feel so bereft? I mean, I must be getting as loony as my friend Lucile. Well, I think she hates me now because she threw up inside her clothes and I had to put her in the shower and take her home, and this was really disturbing, because I think it is a terrifying thing for somebody to throw up inside her clothes, and she begged me not to tell her mom, but now her mom thinks it's all my fault and is going to tell my dad, who says he's coming back from Frankfurt so we can all go camping together, of all the stupid things, and so I probably won't get to go to Italy after all, even if I didn't have to take swimming again next fall. Not that that makes much difference. I seemed doomed to fail American literature anyway, because I can't finish this stupid paper on Holden Caulfield. It's Jake's fault, really; but no, I take that back, but still it is a fact that when I went to leave Jake with his father, here he is coming down the hall with Miss Denver wrapped around him like a garden hose and wondering why I don't submit *Test Patterns* to the show at the Art Institute, when I've totally ruined the thing! I mean, seriously! Maybe I am into total dumbness like Jake says, and worthy of his contempt, and so I won't get to go to Tuscany and roam the hills with my box easel, and this is all true, or most of it is, except for the part about my mother's boyfriend, and it isn't fair, because all I was supposed to do was show a little maturity!"

 And then the wave breaks and great quantities of salty tears are pouring out of my eyes and nose and down my throat. No, this is too much for simple tears. I think my brain must have dissolved.

Dr. Metcalf is staring at me with his mouth wide open, but he recovers enough to push a box of tissues at me. As if something less than sandbags will do. I blow my nose a couple of times. The stuff is practically running down my sleeves. I feel wonderful. Absolutely marvelous. I had no idea that psychological counseling was so miraculous. It's enough to make me want to call up Beth's evangelist and report. And to think I've been going around telling people it was all quackery. I have to blow my nose again, with shame this time.

There is a knock on the door and Dr. Korbel sticks her head in. "There you are, Celine. Jacob's all finished now . . ." She blinks rapidly as she takes in the scene, and then adds, "Oh, I'm sorry, Morris. I didn't realize

. . ." She closes the door discreetly. We can almost hear her tiptoeing away.

I blow my nose one last time and try to become businesslike. "Thank you very much, Dr. Metcalf. It has certainly been a revelation talking to you," I say, getting up. "Yours must certainly be a very rewarding profession, and if I'm ever unable to paint, I will certainly consider it." I have gathered all my used tissues into a single ball, when I'm suddenly inspired. I am familiar with the experience from my work.

"Are you a real doctor? I mean, do you have letter paper that says 'Dr. So-and-so'?"

Dr. Metcalf gives his head a shake as if to clear it and then looks around his office. The filing cabinets, the desk, the handsome pen-and-pencil set must reassure him, because he nods cautiously.

"Oh, that's great. Do you think you could please write me a letter, then? Just say Celine Morienval is excused from swimming for the entire semester for reasons of personal health."

"Swimming? You want me to . . . to write some sort of . . ."

"Yes. Wouldn't that be ethical? I mean, I really do have this terrible fear of water in large quantities. It's my mother's fault. Can I say that, even though I forgive her completely? She just didn't know. What happened is this hospital gave her this baby without any instructions or anything and she had to rely on the magazine that came with the diaper service, and so this terrible thing happened. I mean, it was so terrible that I've repressed completely all memory of it. It was that traumatic. Anyway . . ." As I warm to my subject I notice that Dr. Metcalf and I are beginning to lean toward one another across the desk, our eyes dilating in unison.

"Stop!" he cries, throwing up his hands. He has gone red in the face, as if he couldn't get enough air. I don't know what to do. I wonder if he thinks I'm making things up.

"Maybe hypnosis would help," I suggest feebly. "You know. I could regress in my mind back to that awful moment. Of course, I didn't know how to talk then, but . . ."

"Hold it, I said! I give up!"

"Excuse me?"

"I give up. Surrender."

"Oh," I say, not sure what he's talking about. I might ask, but I don't want to disturb him, because he is taking out a sheet of paper and unscrewing the cap from his fountain pen. A fiendish chuckle escapes his lips as he writes, and I suddenly want to chuckle fiendishly, too, but a flinty glance warns me that this would be the wrong thing to do.

He asks me how to spell my name.

"Will this do?" he asks when he has finished.

I quickly scan the note. "Oh, yes. Thank you very much," I say, backing toward the door. "This is perfect. That bit about phobias . . . How did you know? I can't tell you how reassuring it is to know that there are people like you willing to help troubled children. I'm sure you'll be able to help Sunshine, and I hope you won't think I'm being a busybody if I say that in my opinion the place to begin is with her mother. I shall certainly recommend you to all my friends. Maybe you can help Lucile so she won't throw up in her clothes anymore . . ." I realize that I'm beginning to babble, but Dr. Metcalf is so sternly amused that it seems important to fill the silence until I can get the door closed.

(200)

I find Dr. Korbel at the receptionist's desk writing out a blue card for Jacob's next appointment and Jacob cozying up to Sunshine at the Coke machine. He is such a little traitor.

"Here you are, Celine," she says, thrusting the card into my moist hand. "Tell Mrs. Barker to give me a ring if the time is inconvenient. Remind her, too, that it's important for parents to participate. Vital, I should say." She watches in a kindly fashion as I tuck the card away in my jeans and wonder how I'm going to explain to Mrs. Barker about these vital things.

"Have you known Jacob long, Celine?"

"No. Just a couple of weeks, actually. Is everything okay?"

"Oh, yes. He's beginning to act out a bit, but I think that's a good thing. You seem to have made a big impression on him. He talks about you a lot."

"Oh, yeah. Well, he's kind of mad at me right now, but . . ."

Dr. Korbel laughs. "I don't think he can be too mad. He quotes you as an authority on all things."

"Really?"

"Yes, really."

Wow, I think, going to collect Jacob before he can be corrupted by Sunshine. This is sort of a Good Psychology seal of approval, isn't it? I must be doing something right. Have a way with children. Skillful at guiding them through the complexities of the world.

"Can we lend her some money?" Jacob asks, meaning Sunshine. "She has to catch a cab somewhere."

"No."

"Why not? She'd pay it back."

"Come on, you little jerk," I explain.

THIRTEEN/

We walk home from the mental-health clinic along the lake. The wind is full of spring; the first boats put out in the yacht basin rise in the chop and tug at their moorings. Jake doesn't say much, but I don't think he's really mad at me anymore. He's simply savoring that sweet sadness when the anger is all gone but one hasn't quite decided to make up. I'm happy again. I'm not sure why. It's not as if I had my life in perfect working order. I have Dr. Metcalf's note, it's true, but there's still my paper to write, and the camping trip with my dad and Catherine to be gently sabotaged. The thing is, the pressure seems to be gone. I feel instead a terrific restlessness. Energy popping out of my fingertips. I have to stretch my arms and spin along the promenade in stately circles. I feel I stretch so much that I will never be the same size again. Jake watches me for a moment and then begins to twirl himself. Sometimes our hands touch as we spin. At the slight momentary contact we lift into the sky like helicopters. Not far, no more than a few inches. We float, carried by the wind.

It is dark when we get back to the loft. I prowl through the cupboards and find some SpaghettiOs, but we're both too tired to eat and I shovel them into the garbage. While I do the dishes, Jake sits on a stool with a stale raspberry tart that he has found in the refrigerator and watches Mel Hollingsford's cockroaches come out to feast.

"Here's another one," he announces calmly from time to time.

I make Jake brush his teeth while I fix his bed up on the couch. It's as much as he can do. He sits with drooping eyes, the zapper ready to fall from his slack fingers as we watch another news special on the rumored accident at the nuclear power plant. He yawns and zaps the TV. Tinker Bell flits across the screen, sprinkling luminous fairy dust. Jake's eyes close very slowly and stay closed, just like that.

I turn off the television and go to the window. The city is very quiet. A car is coming down our street, and when it's close I can see that it is a cop car, moving slowly, shining its searchlight down the dark passages between the buildings. I wonder what it's looking for. Burglars, looters, aliens from outer space . . .

I prowl around the loft, touching things. The telephone, Catherine's bathrobe draped over a kitchen chair, my schoolbag, the tattered wreckage of *Test Patterns*. I touch Celine-Beast on her easel. I have to smile at her.

Coming to life there in a space two millimeters thick and a mile deep. I made that. She is not yet done, but she will be. She and all the other paintings I haven't thought of yet. I am too tired to work tonight, but it doesn't matter. I have the rest of my life. That's time enough.

I go in the bathroom, brush my teeth, and carrying a bunch of Catherine's discarded makeup out to the kitchen, I begin to paint my eyes, using the toaster as a mirror. I'm not very skillful, but I'm not aiming for sub- tlety. I draw broad bands of black eyeliner on each lower lid. Very good, I say to myself. My nose swells in the curve of the toaster as I lean forward to see.

Jake blunders by, sleepwalking his way to the bath- room. I am experimenting with a dry mascara brush when he comes back. He pulls up a stool and watches with interest.

"What are you doing?" he asks.

"Putting on makeup."

"Oh. Are you going somewhere?"

"Into the future. I want to see what I will look like in twenty years. You want to try it?"

"Okay. Can I wear this?" He picks out a tube of pink lipstick.

"Of course. You can use anything you want." He draws pink circles on his cheeks, discards the lipstick, and dabs his nose with green eyeshadow. We consult about the colors of rouge, the shape of eyebrows. We contemplate our reflections in the toaster as we work. We are critical, but calm. My lips are cupid bows, my eyes glitter. If this is the future, I will be a terror, indeed.

"Hey," Jake says. "I have an idea. Why don't I stay (205) with you?"

"Tonight, you mean? You are staying with me."

"No, I mean *live* with you."

"You mean I take care of you, day after day, year after year?"

"Yeah. You're a grownup. You can drive and everything."

I'm flattered by this appreciation of my maturity, but of course it's impossible. "Thank you," I say. "Thank you for wanting to. But you have to live with your mother. Or your father." Or whatever. "I mean, your mother really wants you to live with her. She really does."

Jake picks up a black eyebrow pencil and outlines my nostrils with it. It tickles, but the effect is striking. I glance at his reflection. Big ears, rouged cheeks, sad brown eyes.

"Come on, Jake. Let's go to bed."

"Who did you live with when you got divorced?" he asks as I tuck him in.

"My mom. We went to New York. We had a little place on Avenue B. It was full of bugs, just like this one. I think that's what the B in Avenue B stands for. Avenue Bug. You want to watch TV?"

"No. Tell me."

"What? About when Mom and me moved in with the bugs on Avenue B?"

"Yeah. Tell me about the bugs." The bugs. Yes, I

remember the bugs. I crawl under his blanket because I'm cold, and watch the headlights of a car sweep across the ceiling.

"These were very brave bugs, very confident bugs," I begin. "They didn't wait until it was dark to come out like the bugs here. These were Big Apple bugs. They were busy, busy, all day long. They would come out at suppertime to see what was cooking. They'd jump right into the electric skillet. We had a little tiny TV and we put it on this little tiny table, and sometimes we'd watch the news while we ate, and sometimes we'd watch the bugs jump in and out of the skillet."

"Where was your dad?"

"I don't know. New Mexico or someplace. He's not part of this. Okay?"

"Okay. I was just wondering."

"Don't wonder. Just listen." Jake snuggles down in the covers and lets his eyes go crossed to show how cooperative he is.

"Anyway, at first my mom said that you should expect to have bugs in New York. It was part of the *ambiance* of the place, and all the best people like Jasper Johns and Andy Warhol all had bugs. But then one day she was making hummus in the blender . . ."

"What's that?"

"It's a kind of stuff you eat. Ground-up chick-peas and sesame paste, I think."

"Yuck-oh."

"Yeah, it is pretty yucky, but this time it was really

yucky because my mom found this half a bug stuck to the inside of the lid when she was finished. At first she said we should be grateful that we found half a bug, because we might not have found any bug and then we would have gotten all of this animal protein that we didn't really want. And then she said 'I can't live this way anymore,' and she went out and bought this can of cockroach poison that you paint all around the baseboards and the cupboards with a paintbrush.

"That night I woke up in the middle of the night because I was having these strange dreams and I could hear these sounds coming out of the kitchen. Not loud noises, but these dry, secret sounds."

"What was it?"

"Just a second. I'm going to tell you. I woke up my mom and we both listened for a while, and then she got out of bed and I followed her down the hall toward the kitchen. She was wearing this long, long nightgown, but she didn't have any slippers on and that worried me for some reason. She has real pretty feet, and I kept thinking, Don't let anything happen to my mom's pretty feet . . ."

Jake sticks a few stubby toes out from under the covers and examines them. "Feet aren't pretty," he says.

"Not your feet, maybe. My mom's are, but anyway, that doesn't have anything to do with the story, because when she got to the kitchen, she reached inside the door and flipped the light switch, and there they were. Every bug from the Lower East Side."

"But what about the poison?"

"Ah, well, that's just it, you see. The poison hadn't killed them, but it had made them all climb up on the ceiling. That's where they were. Thousands of them. And when my mom turned on the light, they all started flying around. Did you know they can fly? I didn't. I don't think they did. I think it must have been the poison. It didn't kill them, but it drove them insane."

Jake gives a little laugh. A very nervous little laugh. "What happened then?" he asks.

"Well, naturally we started screaming. My mom started screaming, and I started screaming, and we ran all around the apartment yelling our heads off. I was very happy."

"*What?*"

"Did I say I was happy? That must have just popped out. Actually, I must have been scared out of my gourd. Anyway . . ." But I *had* been happy. It's really queer. I hadn't realized until just this minute, sitting on the couch with Jake, how happy I had been. I can remember my mom scooping me up and dancing around on her long beautiful feet, and holding me close, so that I could feel her breasts through her nightgown, and the cockroaches were swarming through the dark air on their secret wings. We had been all alone in New York City, my mom and me, and I had been so happy because we were screaming our heads off at the bugs together. I loved her so much.

"What happened then?" Jake gives me a poke to start me up again.

"What?"

"What happened then? You dumb or something?"

"Of course, I'm dumb. You said so yourself. You are stuck with a very dumb person."

"No, you're *not!*" he says, and gives me a really fierce (209) pinch.

"Okay, I'm not. Listen. This is what happened next. First my mom locked the door to the kitchen, and then we went back to bed and she let me sleep with her, and then in the morning we went to McDonald's for breakfast and had Egg McMuffins."

"I wouldn't. I would have had a Big Mac."

"Yeah. Well, my mom says, 'I can't live this way anymore,' and . . ."

"And a large fries. And one of those cherry pies that come in a cardboard tube."

"Listen. Do you want to hear the end of this story or not? Okay? Anyway, she must have made a phone call while I was in the john, because when we got back to our apartment, there was this guy waiting for us on the front step.

"He was kind of cute," I say, remembering. "He had black curly hair and blue eyes and was wearing this leather flight jacket that was very authentic. I mean, it wasn't pre-stressed or anything. It was really stressed. Really old. He wouldn't have messed with anything that was pre-stressed. He probably *stole* it from some authentic, stressed pilot."

"I don't know what you're talking about anymore," Jake grumbles.

"That's okay. I'm just being bitter. That was just a bitter digression and can be ignored.

"Anyway, he goes up to the apartment with us, and there isn't a bug in sight. They've all taken the big leap into the wild blue yonder. Well, this guy laughs and my mom laughs, and even though the bugs don't come back, this guy stays. He and his authentic stressed flight jacket stay and stay. He was a rock musician, and soon the apartment was filled with electric keyboards and drums and amplifiers and cables running all over the place, and he and his buddies stayed up night after night drinking beer and talking about this road trip that was always just a week away.

"My mom started complaining about how all this was bad for me and I wasn't getting enough sleep, and then he would get real mad and start yelling about how she was on him all the time and she was interfering with his energy levels on purpose because she couldn't stand to see a man succeed. And while he yelled at her he would hold her by the wrists and squeeze them real hard, and she would stare at him very fiercely, but she wouldn't cry. She never cried. But finally she said, 'I can't live this way anymore,' and she got me my first passport and we moved to London, where the buses are red and have two stories, and we lived happily ever after."

"What? Is that the end? What happened to the bugs?"

"Oh, yeah, the bugs. That's the really fascinating part of the story. We thought we'd got rid of the bugs, but then, what do you think this guy's name turned out to be?"

"What?"

"Bug. Cocky Bug."

"What? Is that true? That's not true!" Jake sits up in bed and hoots. Nobody can fool him.

"No, you're right. It isn't true. But it should have been. Truth isn't everything, you know. My mom wanted to get rid of all these little bugs, and so she just got one great big one."

Jake falls down in the covers, flat on his back. "She should have just stayed with you," he says.

"Well, that's what she was trying to do in a way, but she never could. She always has to have some guy around. Unfortunately, she can't tell the difference between a guy and a bug."

"I can," Jake says. "I would just stay with you."

"Would you really?"

"Yeah," he says, and leans up against my shoulder and falls asleep. After a while my arm goes numb, but I don't dare move.

Early in the morning, the phone begins to ring. I open my eyes, discover the zapper in a lifeless hand when I try to scratch my nose. The television is on, but there is no picture. A blizzard of snow. Jake has wormed his way under my arm and one little fist is half curled against my throat. I can feel his breath on my cheek. Carefully, trying not to wake him up, I disentangle myself and go to answer the phone.

"Catherine? Is that you?" a familiar voice says.

"Hi, Mrs. Barker. This is Celine. Catherine isn't here

right now." I blink at shadows. The familiar furniture lurches into stability around me.

"Well, is Jacob there? I just talked to Paul, and he said Jacob was with you. What's going on? Is he there? Do you have him?"

"Yes. He's okay. He's right here. I think he's still asleep."

"Well, what in God's name have you been doing? Didn't you realize that I'd be frantic? Why didn't you call me right away?"

"I didn't know where you were, Mrs. Barker."

"But you saw Paul. He says that he saw both you and Jacob. Why didn't you tell him what was going on?"

"Well . . . it didn't seem the right time."

"The right time? It didn't seem the right time?"

"Right. It didn't seem the right time." Why is she making these little gasping noises? I wonder. It's a pretty simple idea. I mean, I have this vital message for her from Dr. Korbel, and I'm supposed to tell her that under certain circumstances Mr. Barker is going to break her neck, but I'm not saying a word now. It's not the right time.

Mrs. Barker finds her voice. "Don't you realize, Celine, how frightening this has been for me? How irresponsible you've been?"

"Oh. Well. I'm sorry about you being frightened, but everything is okay."

Mrs. Barker is not, however, going to take my word for it.

"Let me talk to Jacob," she says. "Right now."

"He's asleep. Is it okay if I wake him up?"

"Yes, wake him up. Right now. I mean it."

As a matter of fact, Jake is already awake and looking (213) at me with very big eyes when I go to fetch him.

"Is that her?"

"Yeah. She wants to talk to you. To see if you're all right."

"Is she mad?"

"Well. A little bit. It's okay, though. It's at me mostly."

Jake gets up and marches off to the telephone. He looks, not worried exactly, but very serious. For once in my life, I try not to listen, but fragments of conversation drift my way.

"I didn't want to stay with him!" Jake says very firmly at one point. "He was with this other lady."

Eventually he puts his hand over the receiver and says, "She wants to talk to you some more." As we pass one another, he gives me a slap on the hip. For some reason I find this very reassuring.

"Celine?" says Mrs. Barker.

"Yes?"

She hesitates. This is not easy for her. "I'm sorry about the way I was talking to you. A minute ago. I think you were doing the best you could."

"Yes. Yes, I was."

"Well. Thank you very much. Jake says that Catherine is away. Is that right?"

"Yeah, but she'll probably be home today sometime.

I don't think she's been having a good time at her conference."

"Well, it doesn't matter. I'm going to catch a plane just as soon as I can and come home. Can you manage until I get there?"

"Sure."

Mrs. Barker takes a deep breath. "Well, thank you again. For looking after Jacob."

"That's all right. We had a good time."

"Shall I call you when I know what flight I'll be on?"

"No, that's okay. We'll just wait here. Should I call Jake's dad? I mean, and tell him what's happening?"

"No," says Mrs. Barker, turning very grim. "*I'll* talk to Paul. Goodbye, Celine, and thank you."

When I hang up the phone, I see that Jake has found a working channel and is sitting there in the blue glow like a little Buddha.

"Is she still mad at you?" he asks.

"No. She's not mad at all. What are we watching?" The voice of eternal hope. Leaning over the back of the couch, I am not impressed. Jake hasn't turned on the sound and we are watching a very old movie in black and white. Women in strange hairdos and snappy forties shorts are talking to men with slicked-back hair. This is really out of the past. Before there was television, maybe even before death camps, nuclear wars, jet planes, pollution. Before the dawn of civilization.

"Is this all there is?" I ask, trying to get my zapper. I

can't stand the security of these old movies. "It's not exactly prime time, you know."

Jake fends me off with one hand, grinning at a little joke he's made up. "No, it's not *prime* time."

"What time is it, then? Miller time?"

No. It's not Miller time.

"What then, Jacob?"

He won't tell me. He simply smiles, keeping his own secrets.

I go over to the windows and pull back the drapes.

The city is still all there. Black and cool against a gray dawn light.

To the east, over the lake, is a glow in the sky. It is either the sun coming up or the end of the world. My dad is out there somewhere. Probably packing his bag in a Frankfurt hotel or stepping off the curb in the rain to hail a cab. And Mrs. Barker is there, making phone calls, making memos and explanations, putting on her hat and coat. It's all very comforting, really. I bet even Catherine is heading this way, little nose sticking out of the turned-up collar of her coat as she contemplates the gray landscape from a bus window. They're all out there somewhere, rushing home to save the children. They'll be tired and hungry. I wonder if I should make some waffles.

I go back and sit down by Jake. "I'm not sleepy anymore, are you? Do you want something to eat?"

"Not yet." He shakes his head, not taking his eyes off the screen. "Are you really going away?" he asks after a minute.

"To Italy, you mean." I consider. Things don't seem so simple anymore. I'm not upset, but I'm not clear, either. My future has begun to look a little murky. (216) "Sometime I will. I don't know when, though. Probably not right away. Will you miss me?"

"Yeah," he says, reluctant but gracious.

"I'll miss you, too. I really will."

"Yeah, well, that's okay. We'll still be friends."

"Yes, we will. And I'll write you letters. All kinds of letters."

I put my arm around his shoulders and he leans up against me. His soft hair brushes my cheek, and I can feel the gentle rhythm of his breathing match my own.

"I'll dream about you," I say, and together we watch the old movie flickering through the past, until the sun comes up and the room is filled with light.